For
Cindy's

Happy reading!

Bitter Waters

Denise Coughlin

ISBN-13: 978-1503272743
ISBN-10: 1503272745

Bitter Waters

Denise Coughlin

Rose Valley Publishing

***

Published in Shelby Twp. Michigan

By Rose Valley Publishing

7755 22 Mile Rd

Shelby Twp. Mi. 48318

Cover by Carl Vitiglio

Cover photography Denise Coughlin

ISBN-13: 978-1503272743
ISBN-10: 1503272745

For My Father

***

DENISE COUGHLIN

FROM THE LEGEND OF PETA KWAY

***

The waves, the waves, the angry waves.

Have borne my blessed away,

And cast me forth all reft and lone,

With wrecks of wood and clay...

Yet shall I triumph for the storm

That sounds my funeral knell,

Shall lands, and coasts and islands form

Where joy and peace shall dwell.

***

DENISE COUGHLIN

CHAPTER ONE

Those who think there's a time limit on grieving have never lost a part of their heart. Those words echoed in Madison Andrew's mind as she looked at herself in the restroom mirror. A song came to her. *Big Girls Don't Cry.* Tears rolled down her cheeks.

Once again Vincent Strickland slammed the wooden door with his fist. She thought she heard him say her name, but instead, she realized it had been a curse. A wave of panic welled up inside of her.

She stared at the doorknob watching it turn back and forth. After several moments, she heard a woman's voice. "Honey, are you okay? Do you want us to call the police?"

"Please don't," she whispered. Her voice was hoarse from crying.

When she finally unlocked the door and swept past the line of women in the hallway, she spotted Vincent. He was now standing near the entrance of the restaurant. She winced when she saw his face. His mouth was set in a hard line. His brown eyes looked glazed. When she drew closer they latched onto her with a steely focus that made her shiver.

She was unnerved by the change in his personality. This was not the same man who made sure the bird feeder outside her kitchen window was filled when she was so depressed following her husband's death she had not been able to eat, let alone feed the birds. Vincent not only fed them, but he'd fed her; shopping and cooking for her when it seemed she couldn't function anymore.

She would always be grateful for how much he'd helped after Nick died. She did love him, but only as a good friend, not romantically.

"Vincent, we have to talk," she said, trying desperately to keep herself from trembling.

Vincent nodded and motioned her to the door. When he spoke the edge to his voice made her shiver. She could smell the alcohol on his breath. "Alright, let's talk, Madison," he said, slurring his words.

Was she being foolish? She had to talk some sense into him! With a great amount of trepidation, she followed Vincent out to the parking lot

On the opposite side of the country road, the northern woodland was thick and foreboding. The scent of pine trees and damp earth permeated the air, adding a musty aroma to the breeze.

When they approached her car, Vincent turned to her. "I knew you'd come around."

Madison stared at him in confusion. The desire in his eyes told her she'd made a dreadful mistake. Before she could move another step, Vincent pressed her into the side of her car, his mouth hungrily searched for hers. Summoning all her strength, she managed to push him away and turned to reach for the door handle of her red Mustang. For a split second she thought she was safe, but he caught her arm and spun her around to face him.

"Vincent, please, you misunderstood!" Madison's heart hammered wildly as she pulled away from his grasp and tried to catch her breath.

Vincent reached for her arm again. This time he had an iron grip. She could not wiggle away.

"Let the lady go." The man's voice was stern, commanding. "Or I will call the police."

"Why? I'm not hurting her."

"It sounds like you are. It appears she doesn't want you to touch her."

Vincent hesitated for a moment. He finally let go of her arm. "You're a *sand maiden,* Madison!" He hissed.

Turning on his heel, he stomped across the gravel parking lot to his own vehicle. In one motion, he started the engine, revved it and slammed it into gear. Squealing his tires, he propelled the car onto the road, sending up a cloud of blue smoke that smelled like burnt rubber. He sped away in the direction of town.

In a state of disbelief, Madison slid into the driver's seat of her car. For several minutes she stared out the windshield at the dark sky overhead, unable to move. Then she caught sight of the beacon from the lighthouse nearby sweeping the sky above the trees. Willing herself to calm down, she started the ignition and edged the car to the two lane highway. Turning right she headed to the lighthouse where she had always gone so many times before to find solace and comfort.

HOWEVER GOOD HER INTENTIONS had been by inviting Vincent Strickland out to dinner to thank him for all he'd done for her in the past year after Nick died, he'd unfortunately taken it the wrong way. The evening had been a total disaster! Filled with grief and frustration, Madison gazed at the lighthouse from where she stood on the beach. The beauty of the sunset lit sky behind it was in direct contrast to the army of shadows that was enveloping her. Doubt, confusion and especially loneliness swept over her.

The lighthouse itself brought back a flood of memories that poured over her like the icy water of a forbidden, yet life-giving spring. Her late husband brought her to this spot on the shore of Lake Michigan, ten years earlier to propose. That day a veil of mist softened the grand pallet of a summer sunset into a view so surreal she thought she was dreaming. Yet, she never felt so alive or awake as she had when Nick Andrews had asked her to marry him and had slipped an engagement ring on her hand.

It had only been a year after their wedding that she and Nick had stood on the beach in that very spot taking in the sparkling world before them through eyes filled with the wonder of impending parenthood. Sadly, only a couple of months later, she'd had a fall in front of the post office and miscarried. A week after she'd lost their baby, they'd wound up on the shore of Lake Michigan again. She and Nick had held each other in the deep chill of a late October evening. She would never forget how the beacon had swept the shadows of the descending darkness as if it too searched for an answer to their loss in the silence of the stars.

Slipping her shoes off, Madison made her way to the edge of the lake. She looked out over the water, waves of emotion overtaking her. She realized a freighter was directly in front of her near the horizon. Pin points of white light outlined the deck of the vessel. They glowed like tiny stars in the darkening sky. She felt her chest rise and fall as a strange combination of grief and exhilaration quickened her blood after seeing the ship. In the shadows to her right, she could barely make out the row of poplars that stood near the lighthouse. With a childlike fear of abandonment she had the urge to run to the familiar trees as she watched the ship disappear into the night. For several moments she stared at the vessel, finally realizing with a start she was peering into darkness. Only the beacon cut through the suffocating cloak of night that seemed to wrap itself around her, highlighting the ghostly trail of clouds above her in the sky.

The sound of surging water on the lighthouse revetment was a small barrier to the flood of emotion that was beginning to over power her. Over and over she thought she heard her dead husband calling her name.

The word came out of nowhere and slipped into her consciousness without warning.

Like a small thorn the thought began to take root in her sorrow. A frightening sense of peace gathered as the vision and feel of the idea grew inside her. It felt like balm to her wounded soul.

Suicide. The idea became more and more enticing to Madison as she turned it over in her mind. For several moments she imagined herself stepping into the lake. She imagined wading further and further out into the surging water until the waves completely covered her head, then taking a deep breath and ending it all. All the pain. All the hurt. And all the loneliness.

The roar of the surf was amplified a hundred times over in the cold night air. It underlined the crescendo of emotions that were growing inside her, reaching a fever pitch in her soul.

SHE COULDN'T REMEMBER, walking back to her car. *What is wrong with me?* When she first opened her eyes, she was shivering violently and her legs were soaking wet up to her hips. She had also been startled to find Nick's favorite song playing on the stereo. *Did I forget inserting the CD?*

Madison reached into the back seat of her car. Finding the woolen blanket she kept for emergencies, she pulled it around her trembling shoulders. She gritted her teeth as a shiver wracked her body.

Shame burned in her mind.

What would her grandfather say if he knew she had thought of drowning herself? He'd died several years before Nick. Joseph Sabinski experienced so much suffering and loss himself, yet had found the will to go on in spite of it.

What would Nick say? He'd told her in the hospital he wanted her to be happy; to find someone else to share her life with after he died. *How can I ever love another man? Nick meant to world to me!*

She would never forget the first time she had set eyes on Nick. It had been a turning point in her life. She'd been caring for her grandfather after his stroke and hadn't dated anyone for several years.

That morning she'd been sitting in her car in the parking lot of the vocational school where Nick taught when he'd pulled up next to her on his motorcycle. He'd given her one of his dazzling smiles and a slight wave. She'd watched intently as he carefully gathered his supplies out of his saddlebags then tossed his leather jacket over his shoulder before he sauntered into the building.

As her days substituting for the art teacher wore on, Nick's sensitivity became apparent to her in everything he did, from the music she later learned he composed, to the gentle way he handled the group of mentally challenged students he taught. His enthusiasm for his students had been contagious. It seemed everywhere he went in the school the atmosphere around him had been charged with his energy and hope. She had been drawn to him in a way she found both wondrous and frightening. It had been frightening because no one had ever had that kind of effect on her. She knew without a doubt she would never love anyone else as much as she had loved Nick Andrews.

Madison felt warm tears streaming down her face. She took a deep breath and grabbed a tissue out of her purse to wipe her eyes. She was wet and cold. And lonely.

She glanced down at her damp shorts. *And suicidal it seemed.*

She drew down the window in the car. A burst of cold air hit her face, surprising her. She squeezed her eyes shut. For a moment, she pictured Nick, and wondered what their child would've looked like now had it lived. She longed to hold it in her arms. Most of all she longed to feel her husband's arms around her again.

Maybe a year after the miscarriage, she tried painting a portrait of the baby, visualizing its tiny face in her mind. She knew in her heart the child had been a little girl. She never finished the picture. She'd been too shaken by the accusing look she had unconsciously painted in the baby's eyes.

Madison swallowed hard. She was responsible for losing their child. She hadn't been careful enough. She'd taken chances walking out on a icy street when she knew she was pregnant. Now there was no one left to call family except her aunt. Wanda had been a good mother to her after her parents died in the car accident, helping to raise her along with her grandfather.

Madison stared at the beacon trying to decide whether she should head home or drive over to her aunt's condo on the waterfront in town and spend the night there. She needed to talk to someone. But it was late. Besides that, she decided, Wanda didn't need to know what happened tonight. It would only cause her to worry.

She thought of getting out of the car and walking to the beach again. She could hear the waves hitting the revetment. The sound was soothing. The lakeshore always seemed to be calling her. It had a primordial grip on her soul that pulled her back again and again. Ever since she could remember, the water, the lighthouse, and the windswept dunes were a feast for her hungry, lonely heart. Since she was a little girl she had loved coming to the lake on vacation. It called to her. It comforted her and it helped to heal her. It had also helped her grandfather with his memories of the Holocaust. Time and time again she had seen a transformation in him when he came back from the beach with his canvas and easel. It seemed he had found a moment in time when the past did not haunt him, when the specter of evil that always hung over him was banished.

Once more, she felt tears streaming down her face as her memories flooded over. Her grandfather had loved the lake. When she was young, after she had lost her parents, he'd brought her to the lakeshore on weekends. They'd driven up from his farm to stay in the small cottage he'd built. Joseph Sabinski had fallen in love with the area around Sleeping Bear Dunes. His cottage had been his sanctuary. A place where he would go to steep in the sights and sounds of nature and to do his artwork. She had learned to paint at his side as a young girl.

Nick had also loved the lake. He had hoped to become a ranger for the National Park Service at one point, but gave that up to teach Special Education. He had especially loved Sleeping Bear Dunes. The National Lakeshore included over sixty four miles of dune covered beach, besides the lighthouse where she was parked. It also included several islands. One of their favorite places had always been South Manitou Island. They'd gone there many times while they were married to hike and camp.

Several months after Nick had been diagnosed with cancer; they'd desperately needed a break and some inspiration. After riding the old ferry across the Manitou passage, to the island, they'd hiked several miles to their campsite. She would always remember that weekend; one of the last real weekends they had together before he died.

The view from the top of the dune overlooking the shore of Michigan had been stunning where they set up their tent in one of the rustic campgrounds. The next day a storm sent sixty mile per hour winds whipping across the island. Their dome tent, which had been sitting on the very crest of the tree topped dune, had collapsed on top of them during the night. She would never forget how she and Nick had spent the next morning struggling to dry their rain soaked gear on bushes. By late afternoon Nick had become sick and was nauseated and vomiting. She had been worried that she would have to leave him alone while she hiked several miles back to the ranger station to get help.

Nick began to feel better after the sun went down. That night they had lain on their sleeping bags gazing out through the open door of the small tent, watching the night sky as the multitude of stars appeared over the lake. In awe of the view, she got up and made her way to the top of the dune, looking out over the water to the mainland to see the most stunning of sights. For several glorious minutes she'd forgotten her husband had cancer and that the world could be both a beautiful and terrible place. Astonishingly, she'd caught a glimpse of two shooting stars streaking across the night sky above them, almost side by side.

They'd made love after seeing the shooting stars; gentle, yet passionate love. They had poured their hearts and souls into each other with each caress, and tender kiss. Nick had looked exhausted afterwards, but he had been filled with peace, as he lay on his sleeping bag watching her watch him from the shadows in the flickering light. It was a night she'd always remember with a great amount of joy and sadness. The twin stars they'd glimpsed making their way across the night sky to some unknown destination always gave her the sense she'd been given a sign from the universe that they would always be together. How she longed to express that brilliant moment on canvas, to capture the hope she'd experienced in that split second of wonder.

MADISON GLANCED AT THE TIME ON HER CELL PHONE. It was close to eleven thirty. For just a second, when she looked up again, she allowed herself to believe she saw Nick standing on the beach in front of the lighthouse. After a very long and painful moment she placed her head in her hands and cried until her eyes burned and her throat felt swollen and raw. Forgetting that one of her nails was broken, she rubbed her eyes. She felt her cheek burn where her nail unintentionally scraped it. She'd broken it in the parking lot when she'd tried to push Vincent away. She could still hear his voice echoing in her mind. And his last strange words to her. He had called her a *sand maiden.*

According to the old legends of the French Voyageurs, a *sand maiden* had been an illusion of the shimmering sand not unlike the sirens of old that lured men to their deaths on the rocks during seafaring days. It was said that a voyager who spied the mythical creatures on the sandy beaches of the Great Lakes would believe they were real and pursue them, only to have sand fly in their faces and blind them.

Desperately trying to blot the sordid and confusing evening with Vincent out of her mind, Madison started the engine of her car and backed it out of the lighthouse visitor lot. She drove west to the main highway. About a quarter mile from the shoreline, where the larger dunes swelled up on either side of the paved road, a porcupine waddled out in front of her. Strangely she'd read somewhere that seeing a porcupine was supposed to be good luck. Coming face to face with a porcupine would be anything but good luck if you ran it over, she decided. She was certain she didn't need a flat tire at this hour of the night.

Madison slowed her car and watched as the porcupine waddled across the road in her headlamps. Through her open window she could feel the rising wind. She knew the storm was getting closer. A shiver coursed through her. It was pitch black outside and she was all alone on the desolate road. Glancing to the south, she could barely make out the dark roofs of several modern summer homes scattered across the dunes in the dim light. Two turn of the century houses, Victorians, which had been part of the life saving station were mere shadows. They had been moved back from the edge of the lakeshore years earlier when a storm had claimed a good part of the shoreline in front of them.

Above her, the moon made an appearance from behind the clouds then slipped back into hiding. The sand that had been barren near the lighthouse gave way to a variety of beach grasses, then scattered shrubs. As she made her way further inland, rows of pines stood in feathery columns against the night sky.

Having come to the end of the lighthouse access, she headed down the two-lane highway back to town. Stark white birch trees lined the road which curved along the lakeshore.

Vincent Strickland's face slipped into her mind again and again as she tried to push it away while she drove. She could envision very vividly the disappointment that had flickered around the corners of his questioning mouth, and then the ugly menacing look that had finally overcome his features when she had turned down his offer of marriage.

Raindrops began to glisten on the windshield as she sped down the road. Within minutes, a blinding torrent of rain pelted her mercilessly as the sky opened up on her car. The dark pines on either side of the pavement took on ghoulish forms as the water angrily beat against her windows.

Lightning flashed across the sky overhead. On its heels a blast of thunder made her jump in her seat. Pine trees swayed crazily around her. Their eerie dance picked up momentum with the wind. She pulled over to the shoulder. Fear crept into her chest. She turned in her seat courageously facing the creepy feeling that someone was behind her, *watching*. Fighting the urge to pull back onto the now dangerous highway, she smiled at her foolishness. *No one in their right mind would be out in weather like this. Not at this hour! Unless a backpacker had been caught in the downpour!*

Struggling to keep calm, Madison slipped another CD into the stereo. She'd found it at a gift store in Leland when she and Nick had gotten off the ferry. Now the music which seemed so peaceful and comforting in the shop was sad and eerie with only the stereo dial lighting the inside of the car. The music was about lost love, she decided, listening to the haunting melody which included the call of loons. Is that why she had been drawn to the music? The cry of the loons was like the cry of her soul against the muddy reflection of what her life had become without her husband.

The downpour subsided almost as quickly as it began. Suddenly a gasp caught in her throat when the dark sky overhead was once again split by a blaze of lightning. There several yards in front of her car, the ghostly figure of a woman with long blond hair drifted across the road and into the clearing on the other side of the two lane highway. Startled, she let out a cry of surprise, but the sound of her voice was muffled by the explosion of thunder that seemed to shake the earth.

CHAPTER TWO

It had stopped raining when Madison finally returned to town and the old home where she had lived for the past several months. Her landlady had left the lights shining on the expansive country porch, backlighting a row of hanging baskets filled with gigantic red geraniums. The sprawling green and white Victorian was otherwise dark except for a lamplight in a downstairs bedroom.

The wooden steps creaked and groaned as Madison made her way up the outside landing to her second floor apartment. Half way up the stairs her heart began to hammer wildly. She noticed something dart along the side of the house. It got lost in the shadows as it rounded the corner to the back yard. Somewhere in the blanket of darkness a tomcat gave a passionate cry. It echoed in the damp night air.

Relieved, Madison managed an exhausted smile as the tom's "catcall" was answered with a higher pitched cry which was unmistakably her landlady's cat, Sophia.

The scent of oil paint and turpentine hung in the air when she entered the sprawling flat. She switched a lamp on near the couch and let out a cry of surprise.

From what she could see, someone had destroyed a number of her oil paintings. Each picture had been mutilated in a different way and positioned throughout the apartment on her furniture. The wooden frame on one painting was splintered. The picture itself had been poked full of holes with a screw driver. It was sitting upright on one of her upholstered chairs in the living room.

Another canvas of a lighthouse, that she had painted when she was a young girl, had been cut into crude pieces and arranged on the dining room table like a jigsaw puzzle. A third picture of a bear and her cubs had been splattered with a colorful array of oil paints. It now sat between two blue pillows on her couch. She spotted another canvas on the fireplace mantle. Pasted to the front of the seascape was an advertisement from a hardware store.

Unfortunately, the painting she'd been working on for her friend Eden had also been damaged. The vandal had painted a smiley face on it and the words "Have a Nice Day."

Her eyes burned with tears and anger as she checked her electronics. Taking a deep breath, she headed to her bedroom to check her jewelry. The diamond faced Mickey Mouse watch Nick had given her for their fifth anniversary was still lying in the box where she'd always stored it along with several of her favorite necklaces. After checking the windows and door again she found no sign of a break-in. The realization that Vincent Strickland was the only person besides her landlady who had a key to her home made her nauseated. She'd given it to him when he helped her move from the cottage.

Finding an old sheet in the closet, she carefully spread it open on the carpet in the corner of the living room. She collected the damaged paintings and placed them on top of the turquoise linen.

The pain of seeing her work destroyed and now lying on the floor like a pile of garbage was overwhelming. The hurt only intensified when she spied another painting lying on the kitchen counter. It was a self portrait she had done when she was in art school at the Center for Creative Studies. The intruder had dumped a bottle of glue over it and covered it with condiments from the kitchen cupboard. In the center of the painting was the letter, "M," traced with a finger.

"Good work, Vincent!" She whispered, as tears filled her eyes.

Glancing around the room again, Madison froze, trying to decide whether to trust her tired eyes with what she saw lying on the tile floor next to the refrigerator. The familiar shape stabbed at her consciousness, taunting her with confusion. There was no doubt in her mind the leather pouch belonged to Oliver Whitestone. He was one of the many local artists who showed their work at her gallery. Oliver was also the founder of the Skyward

Foundation; an organization for underprivileged youth in the area.

Madison's heart began to race as she picked up the tiny bag. The leather was worn and faded, covered with tiny decorative beads that were hand stitched. It looked very old. She carefully pulled apart the tiny strings and looked inside.

Slipping her fingers into the pouch, she pulled out a tiny bundle. She realized it was hair. The bundle of dark coarse hair, less than an inch and a half long, was wrapped with thread. It had been decorated with tiny beads like the pouch.

What exactly was it suppose to be? She couldn't imagine Oliver Whitestone breaking into her apartment. He was the last person in the world she would dream of doing something like this. Oliver's foundation had helped many under privileged children in the area. Why would he risk his reputation?

It had to have been Vincent. He had been angry at her for turning down his marriage proposal. He'd also been drinking. He definitely had enough time to drive back to town and slip into her apartment before she came home. But why would Vincent have Oliver's pouch?

In spite of the evidence, she couldn't bring herself to call the police. Vincent had been such a big help to her after Nick died. It would be a shame to destroy his life by putting him in jail over one night of drinking and misplaced passion. Yet she couldn't take this lightly at all if it was Vincent. And Oliver Whitestone was a leading figure in the community.

Madison slipped the bundle of hair into the pouch again and retrieved another small article. She gasped as she held the tiny object in her hand. Suddenly the room began to spin and she grew faint.

WHEN SHE OPENED HER EYES she found herself lying on the carpet in the living room beside the sofa. The tiny pouch was cradled in her fist. Her forehead was beaded with perspiration and her eyes felt puffy and swollen from crying. She set the pouch down on the end table and turned on the light. She looked around the room, trying to get her bearings.

The nightmare had been so vivid. She'd been standing in a cemetery rimmed by maples. The web of tree branches above her head had been filled with enormous black crows. They peered down at her with hungry dark eyes. A patch of fog swirled around her legs while she stood in front of a tombstone shivering with cold. Each time she thought she was able to read the epitaph on the marker in the dream, the letters had shifted in front of her and the crows began a frightening cacophony of shrieks and caws that left her shaken.

Still trembling from the dream, she stood up on shaky legs and made her way to the kitchen. After getting a drink of water, she walked into her bedroom and pushed the wooden casement up on one of the windows. Sticking her head out to get some air, she stood regrouping her thoughts as she gazed at the sleeping town below. From where she stood she could see that the breakwater at the mouth of the harbor was being overrun by enormous waves that were almost as high as the lighthouse that stood at the point.

She had not been surprised to learn from Nick that hundreds of shipwrecks had occurred along the coast of Michigan before the breakwater was built. One day when they had been walking along the beach near town he had pointed out the remains of an old schooner peeking up out of the sand. They had spotted several handmade iron spikes holding the weathered planks together. They'd also found an iron deadeye hidden beneath the pilings. Nick had donated the deadeye to a museum, but kept a few iron nails for himself. They were packed away with an assortment of other odds and ends he'd collected during their many walks on the lakeshore. *Just pieces of rusting metal,* she'd thought at first, but somehow these pieces of metal had meant so much to him through the years.

A scene from the story about the *Littlest Angel,* a children's book her grandfather read to her when she was a little girl came to mind. She envisioned a box Nick had kept in their closet filled with things he had collected as a child. *Did he miss them?* She wondered. *Did he miss the things of earth he'd left behind?*

Madison stepped back into the room, She folded her arms around her body in an attempt to keep away a chill. Still peering into the darkness, she caught sight of a string of lights on the water. She knew it was another freighter heading north towards the Manitou Passage. Nick had explained to her that the passage, a narrow strait between the Manitou Islands and Sleeping Bear Dunes Lakeshore, was considered both a refuge and a graveyard to thousands of ships that had plied Lake Michigan's waters. She'd read several memoirs by crewmen who claimed the storms on the freshwater lakes were every bit as destructive as those on the open seas. She'd been very surprised to learn that ocean waves with their steady roll offered more room to maneuver and less danger, than the choppy, pounding waves of the Great Lakes.

She was relieved she could make out the security lights from her art gallery on Main Street. Thankfully her handyman had fixed them. Eagle Bay had certainly grown since she'd opened the Northern Cross. Many of the older buildings in the sleepy Michigan town had been completely refaced since then with new brickwork and trim. A string of docks had been erected on the harbor behind the stores to accommodate tourists who came to Eagle Bay by water. New wrought iron benches and hanging baskets filled with colorful flowers had been added, along with cobblestone walks and streetlamps resembling old fashioned gas lights, giving the town an air of nostalgia.

It was only a few months after Nick's funeral that she decided to move so she could be closer to the gallery. The upper flat of the huge home that sat on the bluff overlooking Lake Michigan was owned by her best friend's mother. Anna Burgess had once practiced medicine in Eagle Bay and was still a tall striking woman in her seventies. Eden's father, Jonathan, who was now deceased, had been the grandson of the lumber baron who had built the large Victorian, formally named Burgess Manor, and had been mayor for many years.

Eden Reynolds, Anna's youngest daughter, was her closest friend and had once played in her husband's band. Eden was now an award winning author who had written a number of books for children. Five feet tall with blonde hair and large brown eyes, Eden had an expressive pixie face. Children and adults loved her.

"When I was six years old, I overheard someone on the town council say that St. Nicholas had been buried in the dunes near Sleeping Bear Pointe," Eden had once explained to her with a grin on her pixie like face while shaking her head. "The schooner had wrecked in the 1800's. It had just been discovered again by some scuba divers in Lake Michigan near the Pointe. Within a week of me overhearing this particular piece of information during one of my dad's meetings, my mom got a call from my first grade teacher.

Apparently, as precocious as I was, I'd asked my teacher to help me write a story. It was about a child who wouldn't have a Christmas because Santa had been murdered! Fortunately, after mom got wind of the project, she made sure I learned to write stories for children that were a little more upbeat."

Lately Eden had been busy developing a series of children's books. She had asked Madison to illustrate them for her. Eden was also in the process of planning an art show at her gallery to raise money for an environmental fund that would contribute to the study of pollution in the Great Lakes. Through Minnie, who was a little Native American princess, Eden hoped to educate children about character and respect for the environment.

Eden had done extensive research on Michigan's lumbering history as well as pollution in the lakes. "Natives by the thousands were swindled by con men that would rent their land and harvest the trees, leaving them with no place to hunt or soil capable of sustaining a crop. At one point the land was left a graveyard of mutilated stumps and rotting vegetation," Eden had explained.

The day they had discussed the illustrations for her books, Eden had brought with her some photographs of Eagle Bay after the lumbermen had done their cutting. She learned that the giant Cedars in the Valley of Giants on South Manitou Island, where she and Nick had camped, before he died, had only survived because it had been impossible for the lumbermen to get their equipment to that side of the island.

Madison turned away from the window. She found her nightgown and put it on. She sat down at her vanity to comb her hair, and realized she was trembling. Looking into the mirror she once again noted the purple shadows under her eyes. She winced. Vincent had been her savior when the depression she'd been dealing with just after Nick's death had left her in bed with a complete lack of interest in food. If it wasn't for Vincent she may not be alive today. And it was because of that she knew she had to give Vincent a chance to redeem himself.

Her eyes swept the bedroom, looking for comfort, for something to anchor her in a growing storm of feelings that were threatening to upend the safe harbor she'd found for the moment. The bedroom was a spacious room, painted a rich forest green with lots of white trim and a white carpet. Above the fireplace she'd placed a painting of her grandfather. She'd worked on it several years after he died based on a photograph she'd found among his possessions. The black and white photo had been taken in Poland before the war. It was also taken before Hitler's tyranny had entered her grandfather's young life and caused so much sorrow for so many Poles. Joseph Sabinski had definitely been a handsome young man. Even though he had faced many heartbreaking losses he'd lived his life with faith and determination, striving to find goodness in people and the world. He would always be her hero.

On the wall opposite the fireplace, over her bed, hung a portrait of a young woman she'd painted when she was in high school. She called it *Woman with a Secret.* It was one of her favorites. It reminded her of the Mona Lisa because the lady's smile was secretive. It also reminded her that she too was living with secrets, secrets just like her grandfather. Fortunately, Vincent had left all of the pictures on her walls intact. It was the ones she had stored in her closet, the ones she had decided to give away to a foster home that he'd chosen to destroy. But why?

Once again, she glanced around the room. Nick would have loved the bedroom, especially the fireplace with the hand tooled mantle. They had dreamt of buying one of the older houses in Eagle Bay before he had been diagnosed with cancer. The beautiful accoutrements in the spacious room; the claw footed bathtub and pedestal sink in the large bathroom, the view of the lake from the second floor was breathtaking.

She was grateful that Anna Burgess had offered to lease the apartment to her after Eden suggested she move closer to town. Even though she loved the small home that her grandfather had left them in his will, it had been difficult living alone so far from the gallery on the small lake outside of town. And there had been too many memories to deal with.

Shortly after his funeral, she'd vividly pictured Nick standing by the refrigerator with his hair tussled like it usually had been in the morning. Another time, after waking up from a nap, she thought she saw him in the driveway polishing his motorcycle. Several times she thought she heard music in the house. She imagined him playing his guitar in the basement. The constant reminders had been taking a toll on her.

Memories of the small home she'd lived in with her husband for almost eight years caught Madison off guard. The sorrow she'd been holding at bay flooded over her. She looked at her reflection in the mirror while tears poured down her face *Nicholas Alexander Andrews why did you leave me?* For several minutes she sat staring at herself, a woman who had no husband, and no children. And no family left. She realized how awful it must have been for her grandfather when he came to America. He had started over with no one in a strange land, working his way through life with many scars from the war.

Once more, she found herself at the bedroom window watching the breakwater. A group of waves smashed against the concrete wall again and again. Their flying spray shot half way up the sixty foot tall unmanned lighthouse at the entrance to the harbor. She closed her eyes, drinking in the scent of the damp lake air, hungrily filling her grieving soul with the smells and sounds of the swelling lake. She opened them to watch the water boil and dance in front of the wall in a dramatic display of untamed nature.

Chills coursed through Madison's body as the wind poured in the window. She let her mind drift dangerously on the tide of grief that washed away reason. She'd grown up believing in a merciful and infinitely wise God. She could not see the wisdom in Nick's death no matter how hard she tried. For a moment she envisioned herself driving to the bay and jumping off the breakwater into the icy water that would numb the pain, once and for all.

Thankfully, a cold gust of wind slapped her face and brought her back to reality. She shook her head, silently reprimanding herself for her dark thoughts. Her grandfather would be heartbroken if he knew what she had been thinking. Nick would be heartbroken too if she didn't follow through with their plans for the peace park. She missed them both so much!

Glancing at the breakwater again, Madison turned away from the window and walked into the living room. *How much like life,* she thought, *so much beauty that could turn so suddenly, so cruelly, yet be so majestic in its darkest moments.*

MADISON LIT A CANDLE. In seconds the scent of lavender permeated the living room. Picking up the local newspaper that was spread out on the coffee table in front of her, her eyes came to rest on one of the headlines. A female resident from a group home had wandered away during a picnic in the area where she had been parked in the storm near the lighthouse. The sheriff's department had been searching for her for the past forty eight hours.

Madison reached for her cell phone and caught a glimpse of the leather pouch lying on the coffee table. She winced.

The dispatcher who finally answered her call was someone she knew. Elaine Wolny had taken art lessons at the Northern Cross the year before. "Madison," she exclaimed, "you don't sound like yourself. Are you sure you're okay?"

"I'm just very concerned about that poor woman, Elaine. I'm sure I saw her tonight. I can't imagine being out in weather like this. I'm also just very tired. It's three o'clock in the morning and I couldn't sleep."

"Sometimes I forget most people aren't on the midnight shift like me." The dispatcher gave a sigh. "Unfortunately it isn't the first time this dear lady has wandered away. I'll definitely let the sheriff know what you saw. They've called in extra volunteers to help search for her."

The thought of the disabled woman wandering alone in the woods made Madison heartsick. "Let me know if there's anything I can do to help," she began, then paused for several moments, as she glanced at the paintings lying in the corner. Her throat tightened. Once again she told herself that she couldn't bear the gossip if news of the incident got out in Eagle Bay. The thought of Vincent Strickland being arrested sickened her even if he was guilty. She said goodbye without mentioning the pictures

She wondered if she'd met the missing woman. She still saw several of Nick's special education students on a weekly basis. Often times she would run into them at the shopping malls in Traverse City. After graduating from vocational school, a number of them went on to work programs that allowed them some independence. However there were a small number of students who never really got over leaving school, perhaps the only real family they had ever known. School had been their world and the most important part of their lives for so long that the change had been devastating.

In contrast, there were some students who had not only the capacity to accept the change, but the ability to plan another rewarding life. Madison finally smiled thinking of the time she asked one very special little lady who had Down Syndrome what she was going to do after she graduated. The girl had obviously thought long and hard. Amy had responded that she wanted to fly to Paris and become an aerobics instructor. Madison had been tickled by the answer, but even more so when the girl had added she wanted to be an aerobics instructor to the "supermodels" there. She couldn't help but smile again as she pictured the slightly overweight, mentally challenged girl, with all of her sincerity and poise intact, whipping the gorgeous women into shape just in time for another important photo shoot.

"Now that's a job I think I'd like too," Nick had exclaimed when she'd told him what the girl had said. "Maybe I'll go to Paris with her."

She hadn't heard from Amy Coulter in over a year. The last thing she *had* heard was that Amy's parents were moving to Arizona and leaving her in the care of a foster home. The young girl with Down syndrome had made the decision to stay in Michigan because she'd found a job and couldn't bear to leave her friends behind. Through the years many of Nick's student's had been an inspiration to her when she realized the hardships they had endured in their lives.

Madison focused her attention on a small framed photograph on the end table. It was one of her favorites of her husband with his class. Amy Coulter stood in the front row next to him with a wide grin on her chubby face. Nick was standing in the center, his blond hair pulled back in a pony tail, Brad Pitt style. He had a broad smile spread across his handsome face. He was always happiest when he was with his students. Or his music. She knew in her heart that Nick Andrews had been a sensitive gentle soul from the moment he was born. He had never lost the child like ability to see the real meaning in things or appreciate their beauty. Nick had understood her like no other person she had met.

Grief and loneliness swept over her. She wiped her stinging eyes with the back of her hand and turned away from the picture. She made her way to the extra bedroom she'd converted into a small art room. Her easel sat near one of windows that went from floor to ceiling. On it she'd placed a painting she'd started of the lake shore near Sleeping Bear Dunes for one of her clients. She studied it for several moments, remembering the many nights spent painting when she didn't think she could handle another day in the hospital. In the sad hours before dawn when sleep had eluded her, and it seemed her world had been falling apart, she consoled herself with her art. It was ironic that the ugliness of Nick's cancer and the sterility of the cancer ward had helped give birth to the garden of colors that had bloomed on her canvases.

She found her brushes and paints and set them beside the easel. She knew she wouldn't be able to sleep tonight after what happened at the restaurant. Fortunately Vincent had not damaged the painting she was currently working on for a client, except the newer one for Eden's book. Why had he destroyed the paintings she'd saved for the group home? Perhaps he knew they really meant something to her. Even though they were imperfect, he knew they contained a part of her heart.

She set a blank canvas on the table next to the easel. Tomorrow she'd drive back to the beach where she'd started one of the paintings that Vincent ruined and begin another one to take its place. Thunder rumbled in the distance. Madison winced as lightning flashed outside the bedroom window. Seconds later the lights flickered and the room went dark.

CHAPTER THREE

Collin Richardson tossed the bright yellow Frisbee that had landed in front of him back to the group of teenagers who were gathered on the beach. Astonished silence descended on the boys and girls as they watched Collin and his dog resume their run along the shore. One of the younger boys ran to grab a bottle of water out of a small red and white cooler. Afterwards he sat down on his beach towel in a lump of respectful curiosity and stared at the man and dog.

I like your dog," the boy that caught the Frisbee called out. "What kind is he?"

"He's a Newfoundland," Collin answered, as the group began to circle around Goliath.

"He's a sweetheart!" one of the girls exclaimed, kneeling down beside the dog and petting his head. Goliath gave her a quick nuzzle on the face. She giggled. "I wish my mother would let me have a dog. "

"I've read about these dogs," said a tall skinny boy with dark blonde hair, who ran his fingers through Goliath's fur. "Didn't the Vikings bring them over or something?"

"A Newfie traveled with Louis and Clark!" another boy added, "I remember a movie we saw in history class. By the way how old is he?"

"He's five years old. Actually, he had a birthday not too long ago. Right Goliath?" Collin chuckled. "He got his own cake."

Collin fondly remembered the day he'd gone to the kennel to

pick out Goliath. It had been love at first sight for his son, Devin, who was turning six at the time. In the weeks that followed Devin had taken great joy in dressing Goliath in his old baby clothes and wheeling him around the house in his wagon.

"Are you ready, Goliath?" Collin waved to the kids and signaled to the dog to come.

Collin was the first to admit the dog was enormous. Goliath's great head had a slightly arched crown and a smooth forehead which gave way to a clean cut muzzle that was broad and deep. His stature was powerful, and muscular, similar to a St. Bernard's so he was always being mistaken for one because of his size. Collin winced, he remembered very vividly the night he and his now ex-wife Jennifer, had gotten into a particularly bad argument about how much it cost to feed Goliath. He'd defended the dog's huge appetite by pointing out the virtues of Goliath's breed, even reading aloud a paragraph in a dog owners manual that told of one Newfoundland getting a medal for bravery by plunging into a raging surf and swimming out to a crippled ship with a line so a breech's buoy could be hooked up to the boat to save the crew.

Jennifer hadn't wanted a dog in the first place, but had been extremely relieved that Goliath had been around when a burglar tried breaking into their home in Grosse Pointe a couple of years later, and was confronted by over one-hundred and eighty pounds of snarling canine gone mad.

Yesterday he and the dog had traveled almost six miles along the beach. Today he felt like taking it easy, stopping to get his feet wet while enjoying the weather and scenery. Especially the scenery. The lake was a brilliant blue which stretched out as far as the eye could see. If it wasn't for the fact that the water was calm today after the storm last night, Lake Michigan could be mistaken for the ocean, for it seemed just as immense. The way the water and sky seemed to blend at the horizon reminded him of a trip he had taken a few years earlier when he and his wife had still been married. They had stayed in Copper Harbor at the tip of the Keweenaw Peninsula. One clear Saturday afternoon he had driven Jennifer to the highest point of Brockway Mountain Drive in the U.P. The blue sky they viewed from the tower overlooking Lake Superior had shown no separation or contrast in color from the lake below. That day he'd felt as though he'd been standing on the edge of the world looking out into endless space.

Breaking into a run with Goliath trotting behind him they traveled another half mile before Collin came to a stop. He shaded his eyes and studied the shoreline. The towering dunes lining the beach were located just outside Sleeping Bear National Lakeshore. The line of bluffs ran along the edge of the great lake for miles. They perched along the shore like graceful sunbathing giants generating a kind of sensual poetry as they lay white faced in the noon day sun, only to be cast with a crimson blush by twilight when he knew they would gaze up at the bellies of blue-grey clouds that drifted lazily overhead.

"I think we'll rest a while, old boy," he finally told the dog, after feeling sweat bead up on his brow. Dropping down on the sandy beach, Collin cradled his back against a large driftwood log and stared at the water. For several minutes he sat there watching Goliath as the dog splashed around in the lake. Finally he picked up a piece of wood and tossed it. The dog happily retrieved it, setting it down near his feet. He had taught Goliath how to fetch his slippers. Now that Jennifer had left he was working on training the dog to get retrieve his dirty laundry.

Collin sighed, remembering his father's comments when he'd told him about Goliath's latest training program. "You're a real character," his dad had exclaimed, displaying a hint of mischief and a good deal of sorrow in his gray eyes, If you would've *treated* your wife right you'd wouldn't have to bother with the dog."

With a bit of surprise he realized he hadn't talked to his father in over a month. He was sure his mother was probably going crazy having him around all day. He was the first to admit his dad was eccentric. He once announced that he loved factories because they were grimy, cavernous places, which reminded him of the coal mines back home in England where he'd been born.

Like all good Englishmen who loved to share a story over a glass of ale, he knew his father had his favorite. He had sworn to many an unwary listener that he'd experienced the ghostly presence of one of the unfortunate canaries that the miners had put deep in the mines to test for dangerous gases. Collin shook his head at the absurdity. He knew Jennifer believed in ghosts too. It wasn't surprising considering the fact she also believed in fairy tales and constantly complained about their imperfect marriage.

He knew their relationship had been in trouble from the beginning of their marriage, but eventually it seemed they became two clashing entities wanting to destroy each other over the smallest matter.

Collin closed his eyes for a moment and let out a breath. He was just starting to relax and actually began to nod off when he heard a whine and felt cold water splash on his cheek which shook him out of his reverie. A very wet hairy face nuzzled his arm. A moment later there was a bark and then another.

"What's the problem? You're acting like a slave driver, mutt." Collin studied the scenery around him, looking for the cause of the dog's behavior. There were several people sunbathing to the north, perhaps a hundred yards away. He could see children in the water close to shore, near the sunbathers. In the distance, at the entrance to the harbor, where the sea walls jutted out in the lake, brightly colored dots lined the concrete wall; fishermen enjoying a beautiful Sunday afternoon. It was obvious Goliath just wanted to play. Ignoring the dog, Collin closed his eyes again.

Five minutes later, after going over his divorce for the third time, he opened them and looked around for Goliath. The dog had disappeared.

CHAPTER FOUR

Madison could hear someone calling on the beach. The sound seemed to drift with the breeze from the lake. With a sigh, she set her paintbrush down and took a bite of her sandwich. The bologna was warm and felt like rubber in her mouth. She tried to swallow, wishing she'd remembered to bring something to drink. The bread stuck in her throat, bringing tears to her eyes as it went down in a lump. A herring gull landed near her not more than a couple of yards away.

"Are you trying to intimidate me?" she admonished the seagull when it took a couple of steps closer and met her eyes with a ravenous stare. "Well you don't have to." She tore the sandwich into pieces and tossed it to the aggressive bird.

Madison watched the overly plump bird devour the bread for a few minutes before glancing at her watch. She was nestled into a sort of hollow amidst a ridge of smaller dunes that were rimmed by a variety of small trees and bushes giving her a sense of privacy. Most of the bathers kept to the north end of the beach, near town. From where she had set up her equipment she could make out the large tree-topped sandy bluffs that ran along the shoreline which was the background in her painting. She had driven to this spot along the sandy trail many times to picnic with Nick and sometimes just to be alone and think.

In the distance, she noticed the dark shadow of a cloud pass over the face of one of the dunes. It made her shiver. She thought of Vincent Strickland. *I will definitely have to change the locks!*

She had a set of extra deadbolts on the door so she wasn't worried about someone breaking in at night, but he had access to the apartment whenever she was gone now. She was still torn about calling the sheriff. Had Vincent accidentally dropped the pouch on her floor or had he done it on purpose? Why did he have Oliver's pouch, assuming it *was* Oliver's?

Vincent had joined Nick's band Cruise Control as a guitarist several years before. He had become quite fond of playing at the benefits given on behalf of the mentally challenged students from Nick's school. She had been delighted to learn that he had volunteered to teach music to some of the disadvantaged youth in the area through Oliver's foundation. Vincent had gone out of his way to help Nick when his health was failing. Many evenings he would visit just to talk and help Nick with repairs and yard work to lighten his load. When Nick died he had been there for her in so many ways; a shoulder to cry on, a helpmate. She had depended on him for so much, not realizing that he was falling in love with her. She shook her head and took a deep breath. How could she be so blind to his feelings for her?

The climbing afternoon heat seemed to magnify her frustration when she thought of the bottled water she'd left sitting on her kitchen counter in her haste to get out the door. Without thinking, she tossed the small paintbrush she had in her hand at the canvas she'd been working on. She realized too late that the brush still had some cerulean blue paint on it. It left a mark on the picture.

Shaking her head at her blunder, Madison closed her eyes, and settled back into her chair. She tried to concentrate on the voices of children in the distance. They were happy sounds that triggered memories of summers past when the reality of Nick's death had seemed as distant and surreal as the brilliant sunsets which had unfurled over the lake at the close of day. A sob caught in her throat as an image of her husband formed in her mind. She could see the muscles on Nick's tanned body glistening with moisture. She envisioned his pale blue eyes, almost luminous against his dark skin twinkling with mischief as he strode towards her with a child's plastic pail filled with water. She remembered the shivers that had erupted when the cold water had met the heat of her exposed skin, as she lay on the blanket sunning herself one summer afternoon. They had been a prelude to the exquisite shivers that had burned through her entire body later that evening when she and Nick had made love on the beach after watching the sun go down. .

Several moments passed before she opened her eyes and brushed away the ever present tears. When she looked up again, her heart skipped a beat and adrenaline shot through her system. It looked like a black bear was coming out of the bushes in front of her. Seconds later, she let out a sigh of relief when she realized it was a dog, one of the largest dogs she had ever seen. Seconds later, she heard a man's voice calling near the shore. At the sound, the dog stopped moving and stood watching her.

Relieved that she wasn't facing a bear, she gave a nervous laugh. The dog finally lumbered up to her, wagging its tail. She ran her hand through the thick black fur on top of its head. Seconds later a man slipped through the vegetation.

The man was obviously out of breath. The way his brown eyes slanted down a bit made him look sleepy. He had a mane of thick sun lightened brown hair with a few streaks of gray in it. There was a bit of stubble on his chin giving his handsome face a salty sea captain look. She guessed he was in his late thirties or early forties. He kept himself in very good shape.

"I'm really sorry for the intrusion," he exclaimed, trying to catch his breath.

At the sound of his voice, the dog turned to look at him and bumped into the easel. Madison let out a gasp. *She hadn't tightened the clamps on her painting!*

The man lunged for the falling canvas, catching it only seconds before she guessed it would have slipped into the sand. Fumbling awkwardly with the wet painting, he positioned it on the easel. He stood back and let out a breath. Finally raising his hands to look at them he winced. Oil paint stained the tips of his fingers. When he realized he'd left dark smudges on the outside edges of the canvas his features darkened. "I guess you've got my finger prints now if you want to press charges," he exclaimed smiling sheepishly. "What can I possibly do to make this up to you?"

"I think I can work the smudges off with some turpentine," Madison said, trying to reassure him. She gestured to the dog. "Can I ask what kind he is?"

The man shook his head and sighed. "At the moment, I'd say

he's a very large *klutz*, fast becoming a total nuisance all in one day!" He paused. "Goliath is a Newfoundland. People mistake him for a black St. Bernard." He finally gave her a broad smile. "St. Bernard's are much larger, though."

"When I first saw him walk out of the bushes, I thought he was a black bear."

"I'm really sorry about all of this. I'd like to compensate you in some way."

"Please just tell your friends about my gallery. It's called the Northern Cross. It's on Main Street in town."

"Are you the owner?"

"Yes, I am. The gallery's been around for about ten years now. I sell paintings and sculptures from local artists as well as my own work. I also give art classes."

"How long have you been painting?"

Madison looked away for a moment. She felt his eyes on her, studying her. "I actually started painting when I was a child." She turned back to him and felt moisture spring to her own eyes. *Why did it seem everything made her cry lately?*

"I'd like to buy the painting when you're finished."

He started to say something else when the dog lumbered past him pressing up against his leg on its way back through the bushes. Rather comically he hopped side-ways to regain his balance. He ignored the dog while he kept his focus on her.

Madison couldn't help smiling at the dog's antics. She loved Lassie movies as a child, but she couldn't imagine life with a dog as enormous as Goliath. She'd always been afraid of large dogs when she was growing up. She squinted into the man's attractive brown eyes, studying his face. His features were very striking. For a moment she had the urge to ask him he would pose for a quick sketch, and then thought better of it. He would think she was coming on to him. That was the last thing she needed.

"This one's actually promised to someone . . . that *is* if I can ever get it finished," she said wincing at the memory of finding her paintings destroyed the night before."

"How long have you been working on it?"

She took a breath. "This is actually a duplicate of a picture. I started the original last year. I had a problem with the first one," she added, feeling her throat tighten. She thought of all the sleepless nights she'd spent painting at two in the morning when she couldn't sleep while Nick was in the hospital. For a moment she gazed at the towering bluffs behind her. They looked eternal. She knew how fragile they really were. Even as a child she was always aware of how fragile everything and everyone was around her.

"What did you have a problem with?" he asked.

When she glanced at him again, she caught him studying her like he did her canvas. Just as she began to speak, she heard a dog barking near the shore.

"I better go," the man said. He gave her a slight wave and slipped quietly into the thicket.

CHAPTER FIVE

Collin made his way back to the lakeshore through the tangle of tree sized shrubs and beach grass. He spotted Goliath standing on the shore about a hundred yards away barking at something in the water. The fur on the dog's neck bristled while the sun cast a velvety sheen to the animal's rich black coat, accenting his powerful muscles. He broke into a run.

Stopping a few feet away from Goliath, Collin studied the lake. A slight breeze made gentle ripples on the surface, causing it to shimmer in the afternoon sun. In the distance, he could see the toy-like form of an ocean-going tanker near the horizon. There was no one or nothing directly in front of them. He scanned the beach to the north and south. He spied a few sunbathers and some children building a sandcastle. There were several people in the water swimming near them, but he doubted Goliath would be barking at someone so far away.

The dog finally stopped barking and began to pace back and forth along the edge of the shore. Once more Collin studied the water, looking for anything that would explain the dog's agitation. The only movement he detected came from a herring gull that landed on the glistening surface.

Without warning, Goliath began to dig, sending a shower of sand flying out from behind his massive body. A few moments later he let out a howl that sent shivers down Collin's spine.

"Goliath! Have you lost your mind?!" He gave the dog the signal for sit. Surprisingly Goliath planted his bottom in the sand

and cocked his head to the side. He finally wagged his tail.

"Don't look at me like you didn't notice me standing here. I could understand your concern if I saw someone drowning. If that were the case, I'd expect a little more out of you than just the sound effects! But there's no one out there!"

Behind him he heard a voice. "I really don't think you're giving him enough attention."

"Perhaps I should pay for art lessons," he offered the artist with a smile as she walked up beside him. "I'm really sorry about what happened." He paused for a moment. "I'd like to make it up to you, somehow. Perhaps I could take you out to lunch sometime?"

Madison shook her head. "It's really not as bad as it looked." She shielded her eyes with her hand and studied the lake. "When I was walking down here, I thought I saw a shadow in the water. I'm sure there's something about forty feet out from shore. Do you think that's what your dog is barking at?"

Collin squinted in the direction she now pointed. Sunlight on the surface of the water made it difficult to see. Fortunately, seconds later, the sun was partially hidden behind a cloud, drawing an opaque curtain on the dazzling show of light. The artist moved closer to him and continued to point. Her blue eyes were animated.

"There's a dark area there. I wonder what it is."

Collin shook his head when he turned to look at Goliath again. "It could be an old dock that washed away in storm."

"Why would he be barking at something like that?" Madison slipped her moccasins off. "The water is relatively shallow here. I think I'll wade out and take a look." She attempted another smile. "It's probably just a Russian Submarine."

Collin watched as she ran a slender hand through her long brown hair, gracefully sweeping it up off her shoulders and twisting it into a bun on top of her head before stepping into the water. She turned to look back at him and make a face. "Brrr, it's cold!"

When she was in water up to her thighs, Goliath gave another ear piercing howl. In frustration Collin grabbed the dog's collar. Unable to contain himself any longer he shouted "STOP!" at the top of his lungs and heard his voice echo eerily against the bluffs behind them. The dog stopped howling immediately and sat down.

He gazed up at Collin innocently wagging his tail.

Collin let out a breath and sighed. "What's up with you Goliath?"

Madison started to move forward again. When she had gone about thirty feet Goliath once again started barking. He tore out of Collin's hands and stopped abruptly at the shoreline. He began to pace back and forth.

Collin turned his attention back to the water. Where was the artist? He finally spotted her outline in the reflected light which shimmered and danced across the surface of the water. Goliath began to whine and paw the shore.

A sudden gust of wind blew sandy grit into his eyes. He rubbed them and squinted at the lake again. The artist had disappeared! *Where was she?* Thankfully, moments later her head bobbed into sight. Goliath let out another eerie howl as they watched her stand up in the water and stagger from side to side. *There had to be something wrong!.*

Giving a deep bark, Goliath hurled his massive body into the water. Collin plunged in after the dog, watching anxiously as the Newfie swam closer and closer to her. She backed away, obviously frightened.

"Are you alright? he finally asked when he came within several feet of her.

She didn't answer. She gave no clue she'd heard him. The only movement on her face was the reflected light from the lake rippling across the contours of her cheeks. Her long wet hair snaked down across her shoulders making her thin face look even more fragile and pale. He realized with a start that her pupils were fully dilated in the bright afternoon sun. When he took a few steps closer, she cringed and began to back away. It was then he noticed the piece of driftwood she was cradling her arms.

His temples began to pound. "I'm sorry about the dog. I know he can be intimidating, but Goliath wouldn't hurt a fly. I don't know what got into him today."

Madison shook her head. For a moment she studied his face as though trying to comprehend his words. Her eyes darted to the dog and back to him.

Collin smiled reassuringly. Inching closer, he held a hand out to the artist. "Please believe me he's actually very friendly."

When she still didn't respond to his voice, the realization something was terribly wrong overwhelmed him. Sweat trickled into his eyes making them sting. He took another step closer. "I think we better get back to the beach," he whispered, extending his hand.

Madison blinked. Then her eyes appeared to grow wide with recognition. Staring at his outstretched hand she grimaced and shook her head. "No!" The word was uttered with such unexpected venom that Collin's hand recoiled automatically. Badly shaken, he stared at her in disbelief.

Once more Goliath began to growl. In horror Collin realized the dog was growling at him. For a moment he felt dizzy and nauseated. Sweat poured off his forehead and rolled down the back of his neck. In frustration he threw up his hands. "Alright, I give up. Would somebody *please* tell me what's going on!"

The movement sent Goliath splashing forward with a frightening bark.

He glanced helplessly at the shore, then at the artist who had her eyes closed. She was swaying from side to side, mumbling something to herself, holding the driftwood to her chest. He was almost certain she was praying.

Halfheartedly, he attempted to get through to her again. "Let's get you back to shore," he finally said, trying to be as reassuring as possible. He wasn't the least bit surprised when she didn't answer.

Collin glanced at the beach again. He glanced at Goliath who now eyed him warily. A chill went through him when he realized there were seagulls circling overhead. They reminded him of vultures.

It seemed to him an eternity passed while he stared at the dog, hesitant to move. The sound of a splash to his immediate right, jerked him out of his stupor. In a panic he plunged into the lake. He was horrified when he grasped the woman's arm and she pulled away from him, fighting his attempt to help her. Did she *want* to drown? The thought made him hesitate, giving her an unguarded moment to slip out of his grasp. He resurfaced, took a deep breath, once more plunging under water. This time he found her waist and heaved her up.

She felt fragile and broken in his arms, like a puppet held precariously erect by a few fraying strings. If he let go he was certain she would collapse into the water again. He felt a long slow shudder wrack her body after the initial gasps for air. *Was she crying?*

He ventured a glance at the dog, then down at the top of her head. Goliath had calmed down, but was watchful. He could not see her face. "Please, listen to me," he said. "We need to get you back to shore."

Slowly she lifted her chin. At first her eyes were blank, unseeing, but slowly the color and animation returned to her features. A wave of nausea swept over him. He could see something much more alarming than fear in her eyes. He let her go, recognizing his error almost a second too late. Reeling away from her wildly thrashing arm, he barely missed getting the side of his head smashed with the piece of driftwood she had so tenderly cradled minutes before.

Once again she took a swing at him. He watched as the wood arced above him, coming closer and closer to his face. Then almost in slow motion, he watched his own hand reach out to shield his head and strike the driftwood out of her grasp, sending it flying into the water. Like someone had cut her strings she finally collapsed into his arms.

MADISON FELT A HAND on her arm trying to wake her. Reflexively she brushed the hand away and murmured. "Go away Nick I need to sleep." A small impish smile formed on her lips. The ploy always seemed to work. He would try to wake her up again. She would pretend to be sleeping and unaware of his gentle caresses. Finally frustrated and playful he would crawl into bed again.

Nick? She waited for the pressure of his lips on her waiting mouth. The shriek of a gull coaxed her into reality.

Shapes were forming above her, pulling her upward into light. Slowly a face emerged out of the dissipating shadows and hovered close. She clenched her teeth at the sound of the strange voice. A knot of fear tugged at her insides. She realized it wasn't Nick bending over her. Frightening thoughts flooded her mind, yet words were slow to form on her lips. *Nick?* A moan escaped her lips when she remembered that Nick was dead.

"Please, where am I?" she heard herself croak. She started to cough convulsively.

After the spasms subsided, she heard the strange masculine voice again. Was this man a life guard?

"You're on the beach."

"What am I doing here?"

The rich dark eyes above her winced noticeably at her question and looked away. "You don't remember, do you? Well, it's an interesting story."

What was she doing lying on the beach with this strange man looking down at her? Madison finally managed a weak laugh. "I usually remember stories if they're good."

The man was kneeling beside her, studying her face. "How do you feel"

"How did I get here?"

"You don't remember anything do you?"

"I remember wading into the water."

"I'd expect you to remember the dog. He was making quite a fuss before you waded into the water."

"The dog?" She gave him a questioning look. A name popped into her mind, out of nowhere it seemed. "Goliath?" she said, blinking in surprise.

The man finally gave her a smile. Most people don't pay too much attention to me when Goliath is around. Do they boy?"

A great bear of a head hovered over her, its large tongue hung out of the side of its mouth like a wet wash cloth. Wincing, she tried to lift her head. The animal seemed happy to see her. She blinked several times. It was probably just a trick of the sun; she didn't think an animal's eyes could twinkle.

"So Goliath," she whispered, "tell me what's going on. Why besides wanting a suntan am I lying here on the beach with you drooling down on me and what feels like rocks in my head?"

Something about the animal tugged on her subconscious. An image of the dog popped into her mind. The dog's eyes had been different somehow.

"Would you like to try sitting up?"

"Yes, please."

The man took her hand. He helped her to a sitting position. A pain shot through the left side of her head. The landscape went into a spin. Her eyes widened.

She closed them and fell back. She could taste the sand in her mouth. The grit seemed to accumulate on the tip of her tongue. Her teeth began to chatter. She put the other hand to her head, touching her wet hair. It lay tangled about her face like seaweed. Desperate for an explanation, she looked up at the man again.

His eyes were flooded with concern. "Did the world get away from you?"

"Huh?"

"Did you get dizzy? The best thing to do when that happens is to keep your eyes open."

She nodded. She was sure he must be some kind of doctor.

"Where do you live?" he asked.

Her eyeballs rolled behind closed lids.

"Can you hear me?"

Once again she nodded.

"I'm going to have to leave you lying here for a moment, Madison."

Her eyes grated open in surprise. "How did you know my name?"

The man smiled reassuringly again. "I saw it on your painting."

Now she remembered. The dog had almost knocked over her painting. "I'm not done yet," she whispered.

"Pardon?"

"The painting's not finished. I shouldn't have signed it."

"Why?"

"It's nothing...please!" Her head was aching and the sun was much too bright and hot. She tried to swallow, but her mouth was dry. Groaning she closed her eyes.

"Will you be alright if I leave you here for a while? Goliath will stay with you."

"Goliath?" In the distance she thought she heard a baby crying. A mist grew steadily in her mind. Once again she thought she felt a hand on her arm trying to rouse her. Hiding a small smile, she pretended to be asleep. The ploy always seemed to work. The hand tugged on her arm, growing more and more persistent with each passing second. Nick? Opening her eyes to see her husband's face, she cried out in anguish as the terrifying darkness overwhelmed her again.

45

CHAPTER SIX

Madison tried to distract herself by concentrating on the television, but it was difficult to ignore her headache. It had not let up since she'd come home from the hospital even though she'd taken the prescription they'd given her. Rubbing her throbbing temples, she glanced around the living room. The paintings Vincent damaged were still in a pile where she'd left them on top of an old sheet in the corner near the window. Not far away from the mutilated pictures sat her easel with the new canvas she'd started for Eden.

She winced, remembering the painful expression on the man's face when he'd dropped off her art equipment. His eyes had widened when he spotted the paintings lying on the sheet in the corner, but he hadn't said anything. *What was his name again?* She was positive he'd told her. *Why couldn't she remember? She seriously felt like she was losing her mind!*

The only explanation the doctors had given about her amnesia was vague and noncommittal. They thought she might've experienced a panic attack because of the dog. They couldn't explain the physical symptoms like nausea and dizziness other than to say she might've picked up a virus. The idea she had something seriously wrong with her terrified her.

Once again, she studied the painting she had done at the beach in a desperate effort to keep her mind away from her frightening thoughts. The canvas had turned out quite well, considering the light she'd been working with. Yet she was positive she could have done much better working later in the day. *And if I'd done that I wouldn't be lying here now worried about my sanity.*

And hadn't she worried enough? She'd spent the last year of Nick's life in a sorry state of constant worry! Yet all the worry in the world couldn't stop her husband from dying. She would never forget the groups of doctors and nurses who had watched, not unkindly from their sanitized corners and from behind the safety of clipboards and stethoscopes, offering what little advice and comfort they could while she and Nick had fought their losing battle with cancer. They had watched her and she had watched them from what seemed like a whole other planet, understanding deep in her heart that most of them were afraid to get too close to her pain, to her anger at life. *Yes, let's keep it clean ladies and gentlemen;* she wanted to shout at them from what felt like the middle of a bloodied boxing ring. *Be sure not to get too near. Death is not a pretty business. Death gets dirty at times, probably causes germs. And your minds, ladies and gentlemen, don't forget to protect your minds, keep them neat and tidy and safe, try not to let some one else's grief spoil your day.* Ashamed of her uncharitable thoughts Madison buried her face in her pillow. *God, she must really be going insane!*

After a few minutes when the fiery thoughts subsided, she focused on an arrangement of photographs that hung on the wall near the couch. Her father and mother smiled down at her as she closed her eyes. Within minutes their faces began to fade into a misty landscape. A great black dog emerged out of the fog of shadows as she fell asleep. The Newfoundland's gentle brown eyes were soon gazing at her.

Slipping deeper into the dream, Nick appeared, walking along the beach beside the giant dog. He waved to her as Goliath trotted ahead to chase a gull. Suddenly a wind picked up. Golden sand began to swirl around Nick. It twinkled like glitter as it caught the sunlight and settled in his blonde hair. Goliath turned and saw the sand. The great black dog began barking as the sand got thicker and deeper, drifting around Nick's leg's and then his torso, finally burying him. The dog let out a mournful howl as he lay down beside Nick's blanketed body.

Madison woke up with a start. She was certain she'd heard someone knock. She sat up too quickly which made the room spin.

After several moments when the dizziness subsided, she carefully rose from the couch and made her way to the door. Her landlady greeted her with a smile that evaporated after she studied Madison's face.

"My goodness you look terrible! I would've been here sooner if I'd known you were sick!"

"Come in Anna," Madison held the door open for her landlady. *How could she possibly explain the damaged painting to Anna without upsetting her?*

Quickly she led Eden's mother into the kitchen.

"Would you like some tea?"

"If that's what you're having, dear," Anna said, sitting down by the table.

Madison rummaged through the cupboard over the sink. She glanced at the older woman who gazed through the kitchen door at what she assumed was her easel. *Anna's going to insist I call the police if she sees the paintings!*

She knew she was protecting Vincent. But for some strange reason she couldn't help herself. The Vincent she knew had always been kind and caring. It was even harder to believe it had been Oliver Whitestone who destroyed the artwork.

"What did the doctor say about all of this?"

"He thinks I might have some sort of virus. There's nothing they can give me yet. Antibiotics are only good on bacterial infections."

"How long have you had this?"

"Only a few days."

She had the urge to tell Anna what had happened to her at the beach, but stopped herself.

And the dreams she'd been having. Was it starting all over again? She'd had a dream about being lost in the woods. She'd been trying to find her way home in the dark without any light except the moon above her. She woke up terrified feeling someone was after her. Was it a reaction to the home invasion? And how could she ever forget the dream about the cemetery and the tombstones.

She realized Anna was speaking again. She nodded without really hearing what Anna was saying and went to the sink to fill the kettle with water. Afterwards she spread a few cookies on a hand painted plate. The sight of the cookies made her stomach turn. Madison frowned.

"Do you have an upset stomach too?"

"I've been getting nauseous. I'm sure it's due to the dizziness that comes and goes."

"And the doctor told you it was a virus?"

"I'll be fine in a few days, Anna. I guess I haven't been taking care of myself as well as I should." Madison knew she was lying. She didn't believe she would be okay at all.

"I can't help but wonder if you're having these symptoms because you're run down, Madison."

"I guess I haven't been eating like I used to. I just don't seem to have the appetite."

The teakettle began to whistle. Madison was thankful for the interruption.

"Eden, says she's having you over for dinner tomorrow night. She invited me over too, but unfortunately I have a book club meeting I can't miss. She's taking me out to lunch in the afternoon instead." Anna took a sip of her tea and put the cup down. "She sounds excited about something. I think she may have gotten another deal from her publisher."

"She did call this afternoon and ask about dinner. I told her I wasn't sure. I'll call her back later. I think she could use the company. Danny's been out of town for a week.

"Well if you need anything, I'm down stairs. Don't hesitate to call me. I may be your landlady, but you're like a sister to Eden. And a daughter to me," Anna added, getting up from the table. She straightened her skirt and looked down at the front of her blouse.

"This getting old stuff is not for me. The other day I realized I had toothpaste on the front of me. I actually walked into the post office with a big white streak on my pocket. I must've drooled when brushing my teeth." Anna shook her head and gave Madison a warm smile. "Take care of yourself dear, life is short. You have so much to live for." She gave her a hug.

CHAPTER SEVEN

The flickering light from an assortment of candles Eden Reynolds had set around her dining room played shadow games on the walls. The wallpaper, a blend of rose, burgundy and teal, set off the rich warm tones of the table and carved Queen Ann chairs where she and Madison sat.

Madison spread her napkin in her lap. After taking a bite of the salad that Eden had set down in front of her, she put her fork down gently. .

"I've got something to tell you, Madison," Eden exclaimed, after taking a bite of her own salad and chewing for several moments. Eden's face finally lit up with an enormous smile. I'm going to have a baby! I took a picture of my pregnancy test with my cell phone. I sent it to Danny. I was so excited when I found out that I couldn't wait to tell him! He said he's going to be a basket case at his conference now!"

Madison got up from her chair. Rounding the table, she held her arms out. Eden stood up and slid into them.

Eden finally sat down again. "I think we may wait until the baby is born to find out what sex it is. We decided a long time ago that if we had a baby we were going to name a girl Charlotte Rose, and a boy Liam Robert."

"I love the names," Madison exclaimed as she too slipped into her chair.

"Charlotte Rose is Danny's grandmother's name and I have always loved the name Liam for a boy. I also plan on dedicating the first book in my new children's series to the baby," Eden added. *"The Legend of Minnie's Pearl and the Great Sweetwater Seas* is only the beginning!" Eden finally paused and made a face. "I'm happy about the baby, but I'm worried, Madison. We waited a long time for this. I remember all the stories Nick told us about his students and the hardships in their lives. I just couldn't bear it if something happened."

"Why are you so worried?"

Eden was silent for several seconds as she looked around the room and then at Madison. "I heard some disturbing things today. A fisherman caught a salmon with deformed lower jaw. They believe that possibly some PCB's are affecting the sex genes and causing the abnormalities."

"After Nick was diagnosed with cancer, I often wondered if it was caused by something in the environment."

Eden frowned. "Nick could have been exposed to some sort of chemical or predisposed to cancer because of his genetic makeup. There's really no way of knowing."

"I've always been concerned about the things they've been dumping into the lakes. They did a clean up years ago, but I know there are still pesticides leaking into the Great Lakes through the ground water. I can't help but wonder if some of those chemicals are causing my symptoms."

"What type of symptoms?"

For several moments Madison focused on the Corinthian pedestal in the corner of the elegant room. Eden had set a beautiful porcelain temple jar on top of it. *A blackout and a case of amnesia, nothing major, unless of course you counted the stabbing pain in her head.* "I've been having headaches and dizziness. The doctors don't actually know what's causing it."

"I can tell you've been depressed since Nick died." Eden's voice was soothing. "Depression *can* affect your immune system. Maybe it would help if you saw a grief counselor again. Why don't you go back to that woman you were seeing when your grandfather was ill?"

"I've been thinking about it. Linda did help me a great deal after my grandfather died."

"I think that's a great idea." Eden nodded and smiled. "You also need to read more. I found a wonderful old book at a used book store in New York. I've already read it. I left it with mom to give to you. It was written in the late eighteen hundreds. It's about an artist who stayed at a villa in France that treated artists suffering from what they called *ennui* back then. There was a magnificent black dog in the story named Leo. He was actually one of a number of angels in the book which I thought was very charming. Apparently Leo was God's dog. His mission was to roam the country side inspiring artists and writers who search for truth and beauty." Eden stopped and studied Madison's face. "What's wrong? It looks like you just saw a ghost!"

"I met a very large amazing dog on the beach the other day. At first I thought he was a black bear. He wandered over to where I was painting. The dog's owner was, well quite intriguing himself."

"Intriguing? What does that mean? Did you get his phone number?"

"His phone number?"

"Let me rephrase that." Eden leaned in a little. "Perhaps this man and his dog really are angels and they've come to inspire you. Would you let them complete their mission?"

"Eden, please!"

"It's been nine months since Nick died." Eden lowered her voice. "I think it would be alright if you thought of going out to lunch or dinner with someone, Madison. It doesn't have to be serious."

"He did ask me out to lunch."

"What did you tell him?"

Madison shook her head. "I'd appreciate it if you wouldn't *harp* on me so much." She gave Eden a sad smile. "I already have enough problems."

"What do you mean by problems?"

"I think Vincent Strickland destroyed some of my paintings."

"Good grief! Why would he?"

"Because he asked me to marry him. I was totally caught off guard and turned him down, of course."

"Did you call the police?"

"No, I couldn't. I didn't want to see Vincent arrested. There's something else. I found Oliver Whitestone's spirit bag in my apartment that night."

"You mean the leather pouch Oliver always wears around his neck? "

"When I asked Oliver about it one day at the gallery, he told me it had been his great grandmother's. The Skyward Foundation would be devastated if Oliver was in some kind of trouble, especially since he's the founder. Look how many kids it's helped in this state. I'm certain it was Vincent. He had the only other key to my apartment besides your mother's. He never gave it back after helping me move."

"How did Oliver's leather pouch get on your floor then?"

"I have a theory that Oliver may have dropped it and Vincent found it. I think he may have had it with him when he came to my apartment after we met at the restaurant. Whether he dropped it on the floor intentionally or not is another matter." Madison paused. "Eden I feel responsible for what happened. I know Vincent believes I led him on...that I let him think he meant more to me than just a friend. I did care about him, but never romantically."

Eden shook her head. "Vincent sounds unpredictable. Please don't be a bleeding heart, Madison. You need to let someone know about this!"

CHAPTER EIGHT

Linda Bishop was in her mid sixties with short grey hair and almond shaped hazel eyes. She'd been in practice as a psychologist for the last thirty five years in the Grand Traverse area and was thinking about retiring. "I heard about your husband's death. I'm very sorry, Madison," Linda said as she adjusted her glasses. She carefully opened up one of her notebooks.

"Thank you, Linda. I probably should've come to see you sooner."

"Well I'm glad you're here today. So what's been going on?" Linda asked, once again straightening the red reading glasses that perched on the tip of her nose.

"I've been having headaches, and some nausea, besides some very strange nightmares. I don't feel like myself at all. "

"Have you gotten a check up?"

"Madison nodded. "My doctor told me he can't find anything wrong with me other than the depression I've been having after Nick died. I was so bad the first months after the funeral that I couldn't get out of bed. My aunt ran the gallery for me. She paused. "Anna Burgess seems to think I may be having psychosomatic symptoms that are affecting my immune system. She's a retired physician herself."

"Why didn't you come to me sooner? So tell me what have you been dreaming about?"

Madison sighed. "Lots of strange dreams. There was a grave in one of the dreams. I was trying to read the epitaph on the tombstone. But the letters kept shifting in front of me."

"It sounds like a very scary dream. How did it make you feel?"

"It felt like the dream was trying to tell me something, if I could only read the letters on the gravestone."

"Do you think it was your grave?"

Madison swallowed. "Perhaps."

"Tell me something, Madison. . .and I'll be quite blunt about asking you this. . . were you angry at Nick for dying?"

Madison shook her head. "How could I be angry at him?" She retrieved a tissue from the box next to her and dabbed at her eyes. "I'm sorry, this is making me cry."

"The therapist nodded. "You're allowed to cry in this office, you know. How come I didn't see you when your husband was in the hospital? How did you handle that?"

"I spent a great deal of the time painting…at least as much as I could. Sometimes I would spend the whole night working on a picture when I couldn't sleep. It helped to take my mind off of everything, the cancer and all," Madison's voice trailed off. "My gallery and my paintings kept me going."

"I'd say you dealt with your circumstances in a very positive manner. Where others would drink or take drugs you turned your grief into something productive by working on your art. I believe your suppressed anger may be overwhelming you and causing your headaches. Perhaps you've done everything you can to hold it at bay which is consuming emotional energy and draining you."

Dr. Bishop looked down at the notebook in her lap and then up at Madison. "Being such a creative person, you are wide open to feelings and impressions. It's only natural for you to empathize with someone you loved as deeply as Nick." Dr. Bishop smiled gently. "I sense you can't let go of your feelings, because you're afraid by doing so you'll have to face the truth that Nick will never come back.

"Nick was my best friend. It's so hard losing him. So many women complain about their husbands."

How long were you and Nick married?"

"Ten years this August."

"Ten years is a long time in this day and age. But you're still young. I've treated people who were married forty and fifty years, who had to adjust to a new way of life. On top of it, you lost your grandfather five years ago. He was like a father and mother to you, wasn't he?"

"That was one of the hardest things I've ever experienced, besides Nick's illness."

"I'm sure it was. Your grandfather helped raise you." Linda paused and looked down at her notebook. "There is something I need to tell you before I schedule any more appointments. There's the possibility I may have to leave in the next several weeks to take care of my mother after her surgery. She lives in Florida. When I go, I'll be staying there for a while to get her situated in her new house. I promised I would spend some time with her during the surgery, but also afterwards. If and when that happens I hope you'll agree to talk to my new associate. He's a very good therapist."

CHAPTER NINE

Madison stopped to watch her friend prune the rose bush near the white picket fence on the property line of Burgess Manor while Christmas music blared from her landlady's downstairs windows. She finally walked up to Eden and tapped her on the shoulder. "Have you lost it? It's eighty five degrees outside today!" She gave Eden a small smile.

"I am on the verge of losing it, thank you very much," Eden exclaimed, turning her head to look at Madison and making a funny face. "We're having a benefit for the museum in several weeks. Didn't mom tell you? I promised I would help her organize it. I also have to finish a manuscript for my publisher, besides doing several thousand other things around here before then."

"Why are you playing Christmas music today?"

Eden shrugged. "I'm trying to figure out which CD's we should play for the dinner. I guess the Christmas music was mixed in with the others. Eden handed her the pruning scissors "Here, hold these for me for a minute."

Eden ran in Anna's front door. Seconds later the Christmas music was silenced.

"Margaret must be pleased about the fundraiser," Madison exclaimed when Eden returned. She sat down on a small stone bench that was in the garden next to the bushes that Eden was pruning. The breeze in the garden was refreshing. The view of the lake in the distance lifted her spirits a notch.

Eden nodded. "Fortunately, they managed to save most of the antiques and now that we have a new place, we do need funds to renovate."

"I remember a time when I had reservations about Margaret Wickers. Remember the *Zapper Affair?*"

"Wasn't it because she didn't like the noise Wanda's bug zapper made in the middle of the night when she forgot to turn it off?"

"When Margaret lived in the condo next to my aunt she decided to get even with her for the noise from the zapper. She sprayed Wanda's clothesline with a garden hose when she wasn't looking. For several days Wanda couldn't figure out why her laundry was actually wetter after hanging outside for two hours and it hadn't rained."

"I hope that's all in the past, Madison. I don't want to worry about any unpleasant things happening at the dinner if Wanda and Margaret get together and relive old times!"

Madison sighed. "I'll try to keep an eye on things."

"So, have you run across the angel you met at the beach?" Eden asked, giving Madison a small smile.

Madison winced and shook her head.

"I'm sorry. I suppose the only reason I get so pushy is because I want you to be happy."

"I guess I should look at the positive side of our friendship. "I know I can at least count on you not to hose down my laundry."

"I really wouldn't count on it," Eden exclaimed. She gave Madison a playful pat on the head before turning back to the roses.

"Aren't they beautiful?" she asked without missing a beat. "Did I ever tell you that they were originally planted when Burgess Manor was first built? They not only survived all these years through the harsh Michigan winters, but managed to thrive. Mother calls them the Grand Ladies."

"I've always thought they were gorgeous. I want to do a painting of the house with the roses in it, as a gift to your mother, someday."

"Mom told me that the original roses that were planted years ago were given to a young woman by her lover. She stayed at Burgess Manor, in the late 1800's." Eden gently fingered one of the pink blossoms. "Danny once told me that even plants can detect vibrations of love in the very core of their cells and that's why these roses survived all these years. I think the flowers knew love was with them when they were planted. That's why they've done so well."

"How did Margaret know about the young woman?"

"Journals." Eden wiped her forehead with the back of her hand then glanced at her dirty fingers and frowned. "Do I now have a black streak across my forehead?"

Madison glanced at Eden's bare feet and nodded. "I think it completes your earth mother look today."

Eden crinkled her nose and pushed her short blonde hair behind her ears. "Anyway, the village priest kept diaries. Margaret Wickers was able to save most of them after the fire."

"I wonder what else is in those diaries. There might be some good material for you to use for a novel for adults."

Eden frowned. "Writing books for children is more satisfying to me than anything I could write for adults, Madison. Adults don't appreciate the sweetness like children do. Besides everything that's popular these days is so dark and depressing. I don't ever want to write like that." Eden was silent for several moments as she worked on the plants in front of her. "Have you heard from Vincent?" she finally asked.

"I have no idea where he's hanging out these days. I haven't seen him since that night I met him for dinner."

"I spotted him in the parking lot at the Lodge yesterday," Eden sat down on the stone bench next to Madison. "He pretended he hadn't noticed me at first. Then he waved. I don't think anyone was with him."

"It would be good to know he was interested in someone besides me."

"At least it's good to know he's leaving you alone. What about Oliver Whitestone? I've always felt and so many people do, that that man has a heart the size of a mountain. It would be very disappointing to me and everyone else in this town to find out otherwise"

"No one seems to understand people and can talk to them like Oliver," Madison sighed. "Yet I've witnessed times he's cut good caring people to pieces because he didn't agree with them. Oliver is an enigma. My guess is there's a lot of anger bubbling beneath the surface inside of him. I sense Oliver's angry about something that happened in his past."

"What makes people hang onto the past for so long?"

"So many people get stuck in the past. My grandfather struggled with his memories throughout his life." Madison closed her eyes for a moment. "Letting go of anger is not easy when you feel you've been wronged. Anger can be addictive. It energizes some people. My grandfather tried to let go of his own anger knowing only in forgiving would he be free."

"I loved your grandfather. There are not enough men in the world like he was."

Tears welled up in Madison's eyes. "My grandfather was one of the finest men I had the honor of knowing, Nick Andrews was the other. They were both my heroes."

"I miss them, Madison," Eden whispered. "I want you to know how sorry I am."

"Sorry for what?"

"For being so insensitive at times. I feel like I've been telling you to hurry up and snap out of it. Grieving is different for everyone."

Madison swallowed hard. "My therapist thinks I've been having these headaches because I'm angry at Nick for dying. There's actually more to it than just the headaches. I've been so embarrassed since it all happened."

"You've had some major trauma in your life, losing your parents and all. How can anyone expect you to go through everything you've gone through and not have some scars?"

"I feel a little better after talking to Linda, but there's a great deal I haven't told her yet."

"You mean about Vincent?"

"Well, partly. It was because of Vincent I went to the beach to paint. I told you I think it was Vincent who ruined the painting I'd worked on for your book. I actually went back to the beach to start another. I met the man and his dog there. The dog wandered into the area where I was set up and almost knocked over my easel."

"I get the impression you don't want me to tease you about this man anymore. Did he try something you're not telling me about?"

"No, actually I tried to do something to him." Madison closed her eyes again. "I was horrified when he told me what happened."

"Why did he have to *tell* you what happened?"

"I must have blacked out. I couldn't remember anything. He actually drove to the hospital after the EMS people and waited with Wanda to make sure I was alright. Afterwards he dropped off my art equipment at the apartment when he realized it had been left behind on the beach."

"Why didn't you tell me about this sooner?"

"I guess I was too embarrassed. He told me that when I was in the water I tried to hit him with a piece of wood. He also told me I dove under water like I was trying to drown myself. I don't remember anything about it."

"Are you telling me you tried to swat an angel like a common house fly?" Eden gave her a smile.

"The doctors at the hospital think I may have had a panic attack because of his dog." Madison took in a breath. "When the dog started barking at something in the water I was concerned there was someone in trouble."

"What was the dog barking at?"

"We weren't sure. That's why I waded into the lake to find out. There was debris in the water that I could actually see from the shore. Apparently I stumbled on some of it when I was wading and fell in. The dog's owner tried to help me. He said that when he came close to me, my eyes had been dilated. It was at some point after that I tried to hit him. All I can remember is waking up on the beach with a throbbing headache."

Perspiration trickled down Madison's neck. "Another thing that's bothering me. When he dropped off my art equipment he saw the paintings that were destroyed. He probably thinks I'm the one who mutilated them in some passionate fit of creative madness. He may think I'm capable of cutting my own ear off too!"

Eden winced. "There is a positive side. If he has any intentions that are less than honorable he won't want to mess with you if he thinks you're crazy."

Madison sighed. "You do know Vincent Van Gogh is my favorite artist."

.   "Well I hope you don't fall too in love with Vincent Van Gogh. I *don't* want you following in his footsteps." Eden put her hand on Madison's shoulder. "Let's get you feeling better! You know I'm always here for you if you need to talk."

"I know, Eden, you've always been a great friend. I don't know what I'd do without you. I thought Vincent was a great friend too. I'm stunned by what he did. It seems like he just snapped."

"Are you absolutely certain it was Vincent?"

"There's no other explanation in my mind, Eden. I can't imagine in my wildest dreams Oliver Whitestone having the urge to break into my apartment and destroy my artwork…unless."

"Unless?"

"Unless, he was angry about something I did at the gallery, perhaps he thinks… oh never mind."

"Madison you need to be careful whoever it was. I can only advise you to call the police. You need to keep safe."

CHAPTER TEN

Wanda Kowalski closed her eyes. For just a moment, as though she were watching a movie in slow motion, she went back in time and looked into her dead husband's handsome youthful face as he smiled down at her while they danced.

Wanda blinked back tears as Victor's face faded into a painful montage of images that made her wince in pain. She could never forget that night. How could one forget such brutality and evil?

It had happened when she had still lived in Poland during the occupation by the Soviets. She had been out late one night past curfew in Warsaw, visiting an old woman who had been extremely ill. She had known it would be dangerous to travel the streets of the city with so many soldiers about, but her love for the old woman and the conviction that God would protect her had prevailed. She had pressed on through the somber weary lanes, almost reaching the safety of the woman's small apartment when she passed an alley.

A group of Soviet soldiers had a young Polish girl pressed up against a brick wall. The evil intent on their faces had been clear. The horror of what the girl was about to experience penetrated Wanda's consciousness like an icy saber.

One of the soldiers turned just in time to catch her terrified eyes in his own. Frozen in her steps as the soldier had approached, she had watched and prayed, but could not scream or run.

Hysterical blindness is what the doctors had called her condition when she lost her vision soon afterwards.

Years later, before she'd left Poland, she'd felt a need to visit the places that were sorrowful reminders of the past. Even though her vision had still not returned, she'd made a trip with several nuns to one of the concentration camps that had been maintained by the Nazi's within the Polish borders. Music was the only word she could use to describe the unearthly sensation she had experienced the emotional vibrations of the past.

In one of the barracks at the camp a very strange thing had happened. She had not only heard, but it seemed she had felt the discordant music of intense suffering as she walked through the buildings on the prison grounds. She had also felt the raw searing scrape of a hunger that was not her own. But there had also been a beautiful melody playing in the background, Sister Magdalene hadn't heard it, but she definitely had. The music had been soft and hesitant, building in tone and depth, finally echoing in her darkness. She was sure it was a song of faith. Whether Jewish or Christian, she was sure the music had brought about the miracle. It was on that very night of the trip she had regained her vision.

Realizing her hands were trembling now, Wanda reached for the bottle of wine she had set on the coffee table in front of her. She poured herself another glass and took a sip of the liquid, thankfully feeling the calming effect of the alcohol almost at once. Strangely it was not only the Polish girl she had dreamt of after so many years. She had dreamt of another young woman who she believed was in danger.

Wanda stared at the clock on the wall for several minutes deep in thought. Finally lifting her glass to her mouth, she felt a drop of wine dribble down her chin and onto her nightgown. Shaking her head at her clumsiness, she got up from the couch and went into the bathroom. Turning on the water she worked at the stain with some soap, all the while studying her reflection in the mirror. She remembered a time when her silver hair had been a rich chestnut brown and had fallen to her waist before it had been cut in the convent. She studied the dark circles under her eyes. The sight of them made her swallow hard.

Wanda walked into the small living room and glanced at the television her niece had given her for her birthday, wondering if she should turn it on. She liked to watch the talk shows in the morning. Yet she often wondered what impact they had on children. She knew television was a powerful teacher. She had often heard people say the box was just a reflection of the world. She was sure the television had been developed to be more than just a mirror, it was a window into the human heart and the possibilities for it to inspire and teach were endless. But the media also had the power to create illusions, illusions that created prisons in the young minds it influenced.

It seemed many young girls starved themselves so they could look like the models they saw on television. She had known of several girls in the Catholic High School where she'd taught whom she suspected were anorexic. One day she had confronted one of the children who seemed to be wasting away before her eyes.

"Teila, why aren't you eating? Isn't your mother feeding you?" she had asked the pretty black girl one day during her history class. Undaunted she had pressed on determined to at least make some sort of statement to this child that might make a difference.

"Teila, have you ever seen the Statue of Liberty? She had asked.

Teila nodded.

"So you've been to Ellis Island?"

Teila shook her head. "Only in books, Mrs. Kowalski."

"I saw her in New York harbor when I first came to this country. She was the most wondrous sight in the world to me. She was a woman the likes of which I had never seen before, nor imagined. I realized when looking at her she was made to look big and powerful and mighty. The lady actually had muscles. Now why are you starving yourself?"

The girl had looked at her like she had something green and slimy caught between her teeth and was trying to figure out what it was.

"Pardon?"

"I can't imagine why you are trying to resemble a coat hanger. It seems fashion designers want their models to look emaciated so they don't take attention away from the clothes they are wearing. "

Teila had looked at her and winced. Then she had given her a hesitant smile, "Alright, Big Mama, I get it. You want me to be a woman of substance."

"With a capital S. Teila. I want no shrinking violets in my history class. We're talking Amelia Earhart here and Lady Liberty; let them teach you a thing about freedom."

She would always remember Teila's smile. She needed to remember it, because she didn't think she ever saw the girl smile again after that day. Soon afterwards, Teila found out she was pregnant. She never told anyone who the father was. But her mother tried forcing her to have an abortion, and kicked her out of the house when she refused. Teila had come to her for advice despite her mother's threats to put her in a youth home. She had been very much alone and afraid and wondering where Lady Liberty was when she needed her.

It had been remarkable how the girl had fought to keep her baby. Teila raised her child into a fine young man by herself. It had been astonishing to her how the girl managed to survive her ordeal with her spirit intact. Why did some children who had all the advantages in the world crash and burn while others who had struggled all their lives in appalling conditions find the strength to climb above their adversities?

Wanda knew it was character. She had read in Time Magazine years before that psychologists were calling it the emotional I. Q and recognized its importance for success in life. She had to smile thinking of all the years the nuns had taught kids believing the best you could give them was a spirit filled with something called faith and hope to tackle life's many problems.

She rubbed her eyes and looked down at her hands, thinking of all the children she had taught in the parochial school near Detroit. *Had she done her job?* A chill coursed through her. *It was a never ending struggle it seemed!* In her mind her religion had tried to bring the development of character to a sacred art form. But sometimes she feared it would become a lost art as more and more of the discipline was fragmented by the secular culture that did not choose to understand its beauty and wisdom. Now it seemed to her image was a substitute for character and substance. Kid's worshiped what amounted to illusions.

Yes, she was very proud that Teila had character and she hoped she had something to do with it. The girl had eventually become a lawyer, a good one at that. When the world was looking for heroes, little Teila Johnson had been too busy taking care of the poor and unfortunate souls on the planet to join in the search.

The numbing heaviness in her heart seemed to consume her like an icy liquid. Wanda felt as though in a minute or two she might not be able to breath. Yesterday she had found out that Teila's son, Brandon, had been killed by a stray bullet during a gang shoot out! She had heard Brandon sing songs with a voice she was sure only angels were allowed to have. Now he was gone. Gone before anyone could catch their breath it seemed. Teila had worked so hard to make a home for the boy. She had been so proud and so careful.

After wiping her eyes with a tissue, she turned on the television Madison had given her. On the Jerry Springer show a husband and wife were going to confront each other about their infidelities. *So what else was new?* She quickly changed the channel. On the Marley Hansen show she found a pair of psychics who had come to the program to help several families with missing children. She was amazed that the women could stay calm as they related such horrible circumstances. There were numerous times she'd been so overwhelmed by her dreams that they made her physically ill. What happened that awful evening in Warsaw was something she suffered with in the middle of the night when she awoke with her head pounding and perspiration all over her trembling body, when the shadows of her lonely bedroom loomed over her like a squad of Soviet soldiers waiting to terrorize their next victim.

An image of her niece suddenly popped into her mind. Madison? Madison was all she had in the world! If anything ever happened to her niece she didn't know if she could ever find the will to live.

CHAPTER ELEVEN

Madison turned the stereo off in the car and watched the road. There was always construction on this stretch of highway along the lake. She couldn't remember a single day she'd not been caught in some sort of work zone in this area. Nor could she remember a day she had not been in awe of the landscape around her. Numerous times she'd wondered what the lakeshore around the National Park had looked like thousands of years before when a glacier first carved out the great lakes and left the golden white sand to be blown into mountains of sparkling sediment near the water's edge.

After finding a space in the parking lot, she walked over to the observation deck that was built over the western face of the dunes. Sand pelted her cheeks like tiny needles as she looked down over the water. She remembered standing in this exact spot with Nick beside her one warm August day years ago. Together they gazed into the crystal clear lake more than three hundred feet below the tower and saw gigantic shapes lying at the bottom near the shore. Nick said they were sturgeon, prehistoric fish that had been around for thousands and thousands of years. She had been surprised by how huge they were. The giant fish had appeared larger than the people three hundred feet below who were hiking along the shore.

Madison turned away from the edge of the platform. She slowly made her way down the path that meandered across the top of the bluffs. She watched a young father who was smiling broadly gather his small son into his arms as she approached. The wind adding to the father's joy of the moment, plastered the hood of the child's red jacket to his smiling face. The man stopped for a moment, still grinning as he peeled the hood away from his eyes, then adjusted the little boy in his arms. He turned to his wife who was walking beside him and put his arm around her shoulders. The young woman gave her a huge smile just as the wind sent Madison's own hair flying into her face. Blinded for several moments, Madison took a step forward, tripping over a piece of wood in the middle of the path. She thought she was hallucinating when a huge black dog appeared out of nowhere, it seemed, while she sat on the ground. Seconds later, the dog's owner came from behind. She squinted up at his face, as he towered over her and the bright sun behind him blinded her."

"Are you okay?"

"I think so," she said, as a dozen images flashed through her mind of their encounter on the beach. Reaching for the man's outstretched hand; she avoided looking at him as he helped her to a standing position. When she was on her feet again, the dog came up to her and nuzzled her arm.

"How's Goliath been?" She ran her fingers through the thick fur on top of the dog's massive head.

The man held up a dog leash and smiled. "Goliath is still on probation today." He gave her a small nod. "And how have you been?"

"I'm feeling a bit better. Thanks for asking."

"I still would like to compensate you for the painting Goliath knocked over."

"There were only a few smudges on the side. I was able to remove them with some turpentine." She took a breath and paused for a moment before she continued, "I could tell you were a little upset when you were at my apartment and saw the other paintings that were lying in the corner," she added"

He glanced down at her foot. "Are you sure you can walk?"

"I don't think I'll have any problems," she said softly.

"Have you been back to the beach again to paint?"

Madison shook her head. "Actually I've been trying to recuperate from whatever's been making me feel so bad lately.

"I hope you'll feel better soon." He paused for a moment. "By the way, I did get a chance to visit your gallery last week. I had a chat with your aunt. She seems like a very nice woman. I plan on buying one of your paintings for my office, that is, if I can decide which one. They are all very beautiful."

"Thank you," she said, as she brushed her hair away from her face and gave him a smile. "The Northern Cross is open six days a week during the summer. If you plan to come in again, let me know when, and I'll show you around myself. Are you going back to your car? I think I better go back too."

They walked side by side in silence for several minutes. When she realized they were approaching the parking lot, a feeling of relief came over her.

"I see a picnic table over there. I actually packed some extra food today," the man said, as they approached the cars. Would you like to join Goliath and me for lunch?"

She could tell he was trying very hard to put her at ease. But at the moment, his steady gaze made her extremely nervous. He always seemed to be studying her. *He was probably trying to decide whether she might try to hit him again.*

"I really don't think…"

Before she could finish her sentence Goliath began to whine.

"Would you mind holding the leash for a minute while I get some things out of my trunk? We can eat over there where it's sheltered from the wind."

Resigned to the fact that she would feel she was being extremely rude to someone who had gone above and beyond the call of duty to help her, if she didn't take him up on his offer, she walked over to a nearby picnic table with the dog while he rummaged in the trunk of his car. She watched Goliath sniff under the tree near the table for a few minutes before she sat down. Goliath gave several quick barks as he focused on a chipmunk that scurried back and forth across the grass near him. The dog finally laid down under the tree when the chipmunk disappeared.

"Micro Bears," The man said, shaking his head as he walked up to the picnic table and put a small cooler down on it. They both watched as one of the more courageous chipmunks climbed the tree just behind Goliath to sit on a branch over him. After a minute he handed Madison a sandwich wrapped in plastic. "I'll never forget camping in Northern Michigan one summer when I was in college, and having a hungry chipmunk scurry into my backpack looking for food. I didn't realize he was in there and actually zipped it closed. The funny thing is I carried him for over a mile before I realized what had happened."

She finally gave a small laugh. "Thank you again," she said, taking the sandwich. "What did you do with the chipmunk?" She studied his long slender fingers as he held his own sandwich. They reminded her of Nick's.

"I let the little stowaway go at the nearest bush. He was a very happy camper then." For several seconds he was silent. "Madison," he finally said.

She looked up, startled by the sound of his voice saying her name. She felt warmth penetrate her cheeks as her eyes met his.

"I like the name Madison, very much."

Once again, she was captivated by his brown eyes. The way they slanted gave him a sleepy look and reminded her of a young Paul McCartney.

"My father, whose own father was an immigrant, wanted me to have an authentic American name when I was born, so he named me after Madison Avenue." She finally smiled. "I guess I should be thankful he didn't name me after Wall Street. By the way, what is your name again?"

"Collin, that's spelled with two L's, Richardson. I think it might have been my father's great uncle's name. I have a feeling he may have been a potato farmer in Ireland who turned horse thief." He held a can of Coke out to her. "Would you like one?"

She shook her head. "No thanks. But if you have water, I'll take one." They were quiet for several moments after he handed her a bottle of water from the cooler. He finally broke the silence. "I have a son. He lives with his mother in Grosse Pointe. His name is Devin." He took a bite of his sandwich and looked up at the sky. "I've been divorced for almost a year," he finally said after chewing.

"It's difficult going through a divorce, especially if there are kids involved," she said, studying his face.

"It's definitely hard on the kids," he said, sighing.

"How do you like it up here?"

"In many ways it reminds me of Long Island where I grew up. I love the water. My uncle used to take me out on his old fishing scow when I was a kid."

"Do you have a boat, now?"

"My father and I share an antique cabin cruiser we take to all the antique boat shows. I'd love to have it brought up here if I could, but I doubt it would withstand the trip without being damaged."

Damaged. "About the paintings in my apartment," she began, hoping he would finally let her explain. "I know how it must have looked after what happened at the beach," she said, studying his face. She realized he was avoiding her eyes.

Goliath began to whine. Collin ignored the dog and glanced down at her foot. "How does your ankle feel now?" he asked.

It seemed all the pent up anxiety she'd been feeling since she last saw him finally poured out of her. "My foot is fine! I realize you know nothing about me. I don't know what happened in the water that day, but it's frightening me that I can't remember anything."

Collin nodded "I think you should have someone look at your ankle when you get home. Sometimes you don't actually feel it until a day or two later."

Madison winced. He was definitely avoiding her eyes and any mention of the paintings. He may think he was giving her a way to save herself some embarrassment, but it was frustrating! "How many art classes do you have at the gallery?"

"I hold six classes during the week." she answered, realizing he would probably go away thinking she was a nutcase and pity her. She felt a surge of anger course through her. *She didn't want or need his pity!* "Tell me something. Doesn't it seem odd that I'm not afraid of Goliath now?" she said, capturing Collin's gaze. She needed to hear him tell her again what had happened that day at the beach. She needed to know how crazy she'd been.

"Madison," he said, softly. "Sometimes things just happen to good people. Maybe you should talk to someone about all of this." Collin whispered.

Why did his suggestion infuriate her? Yet she wasn't about to tell him she'd been going to a therapist. Somehow she didn't want to give him that satisfaction.

"You mentioned your husband passed away. Do you have a clergyman you're comfortable with?"

"Would you please let me explain! I think you've been assuming a lot of things about me."

Collin took a deep breath and let it out. "I'm sorry Madison. I guess I haven't quite come to terms with it all myself."

"I don't understand."

"Neither do I." he said quietly.

"Mr. Richardson, I know how the damaged paintings in my apartment must have looked to you."

"My name is Collin," he said softly. Mr. Richardson sounds so formal."

"Collin, I'm concerned about what you told me happened at the lake. I've been trying to come to terms with it. Also I can only guess how it must have looked to you in my apartment. I can assure you I didn't destroy the paintings."

Collin shook his head. "Who would do such a thing?"

"I didn't have them destroyed for the insurance, if that's what you're thinking. The paintings weren't insured. They were old canvases that I've had since I was a young girl. I was going to give them away to a group home."

"Were they vandalized?"

"It's a long story. It all began when my husband died. This person believed I cared for him more than I actually did. He asked me to marry him."

"And he destroyed the paintings when you turned down his marriage proposal?"

"I believe it was him."

Collin winced. "He sounds like he needs a great deal of help himself." .

A great deal of help himself? "I'm sorry I've been such trouble to you, Mr. Richardson!" Madison stood up. She gave him a quick wave before turning her back on him and heading down the path to the parking lot. It all seemed so unfair, she thought. It was a pity life seemed to search her out when it wanted to amuse itself with the sufferings of a woman whose only fault was that she wanted to trust it too much. Her grandfather had always searched for the goodness in life, but today she was having a hard time believing she had not been the focus of a very bad practical joke.

CHAPTER TWELVE

Wanda could feel the worry descending on her as she observed Madison from the back of the art room at the Northern Cross. *She has lost more weight! And those dark circles under her eyes!* Wanda waited patiently as Madison stopped to give advice and encouragement to the handful of women who'd taken the oil painting class. Afterwards she returned to her own easel at the front of the room to make an announcement.

"I want to remind everyone that today is Vincent VanGogh's birthday," Madison exclaimed, attempting a bright smile for her art students. "Last night I thought long and hard about what dear Vincent would say to his students if he were still with us. I think he would tell them that they can't be afraid of using color. Color is what makes the world so interesting and beautiful. I think he would also tell his students he wanted them to create paintings that would make him tremble in awe, like I do!"

Everyone in the art room laughed.

Wanda made her way to where her niece stood. "I have some good news for you, dear. I just was told you were chosen artist of the year by the Grand Traverse Artists Consortium. That's quite an honor. Congratulations!"

"You submitted my name didn't you my dear sneaky aunt?"

"And you deserved to be nominated, Madison. Your heart seems to be wide open when you paint, showing the world the bit of heaven their tired eyes are longing to see!"

Madison wrapped her arms around Wanda and kissed her aunt's cheek. Drawing slowly away she looked into Wanda's eyes and studied them "It looks like you haven't been getting much sleep either. Why do you have such dark circles? They're almost as dark as mine."

Before Wanda could answer, one of the women in the art room walked up to Madison and put her hand on her shoulder. "Could I borrow our illustrious teacher for a minute?"

Thankful for the interruption, Wanda turned to her niece. "I don't want to keep you from your students. I'll talk to you later, dear."

Without further comment, Wanda made a swift exit to the gallery office. Brightly colored posters on the cream colored walls made the room appear smaller than it actually was. Her gaze rested on a poster she had put up several weeks earlier. Under a photograph showing a child's hand resting on top of an older more mature one was the caption, *'No one is useless that lightens the burden of another.'*

Sinking into the chair, she turned on the radio next to her. Classical music filled the small space as she searched the drawers for writing paper.

Several moments later, Madison poked her head into the doorway and squinted at the calendar that hung on the wall. "Does the new session begin next week?" she asked. "I'm losing track of time."

When Wanda didn't answer, Madison slipped into the room and sat down on one of the extra chairs. "Is there something wrong?" she finally asked.

Wanda gave a small nod. "Tchaikovsky was afraid of his own shadow. Did you know that, Madison? Did you know he was so neurotic he was afraid his head would fly off during one of his symphonies? Such beautiful music and so astounding to think it was probably born of his fear of his own sexuality."

"And what is making you so fearful?"

Wanda shook her head. "I fear a lack of music," she finally whispered. "I fear people getting hurt and being unable to help them. I fear people dying who don't deserve to die. And most of all I fear my own inadequacy. Sometimes I dream I look into a terrifying darkness and the face I see looking back at me is my own with great haunted eyes. I wasn't always like this. I was young and brave once. I think time plays tricks on the mind. The darkness seems to take over if you don't service the light." Wanda squeezed her eyes shut for a moment and shook her head. "I'm sorry, dear. I know I'm talking in riddles now."

"You have been talking in lots of riddles lately. This morning you told me that the dream had changed. What exactly did you mean?"

Wanda looked down at the desk for a moment. "Madison, a different girl has appeared in my dream. Several days ago I saw her face in the newspaper. She was one of the girls who was found murdered near Detroit!" Wanda finally looked up at Madison and saw her wince. "For the past several nights, I've been seeing another girl in the dream," she added.

"How awful! Do you think you can help them in some way? Is that what this is about?"

Wanda sighed. "I don't know, dear. But I do know I want you to be careful! You're all I have! I know Victor would've been so proud to have a daughter like you if only we could have had children."

"Victor was a proud man, Wanda."

"Yes, he was a proud man. I often think God is punishing me for leaving the convent when I was a girl."

Madison took her aunt's hand in her own. "I'm sure God isn't punishing you. Why would he? You and Victor were two very good people who fell in love and wanted to spend their lives together. There's something extremely holy in that isn't there? In this day and age we need to see love like that!"

"I'm so ashamed. It seems I've been drowning in self pity lately." Wanda pulled a tissue out of the box on top of the desk.

CHAPTER THIRTEEN

Madison glanced around the therapist's office waiting for Collin Richardson to look up from the material he was reading in the doorway and recognize her. She clenched her hands a little tighter, her nervousness finally overcoming her. *What could he possibly be doing here?*

"Hello Madison," Collin said, as he entered the room and quietly seated himself in Linda Bishop's leather chair. "I can assure you this is just as much a surprise to me as it is to you."

She stared at him in disbelief.

Collin gave her a reassuring smile. "In many ways I think this situation can actually work to your advantage."

She confronted him with eyes filled with the same helpless anguish she had felt off and on during the past couple of weeks. "The doctors at the hospital told me they thought I might have had a panic attack because of your dog."

"Yes, I'm aware of that." Collin said quietly. He looked down at the notebook that was now spread open on the desk in front of him. "From what Linda's told me, you started seeing her about twelve years ago when your grandfather was ill? Is that right?"

Madison swallowed hard. "How did this happen?"

"Linda did ask you if you would like to talk to one of her colleagues while she was away. She must have told you my name. Would you prefer someone else?"

"She did give me a name. Apparently I didn't connect it with you. You're the last person I expected to see here."

"I'm sure this is a big surprise then"

This is more than a surprise, it's unbelievable!" She looked around the room, finally turning back to face him and took a deep breath. "I have to admit my aunt has always reminded me there are no such things as coincidences. She believes everything happens for a reason. Right now this seems like some kind of joke to me. "

"I do understand," Collin said. He looked down at his notebook again. "Linda told me that you came here when you were struggling with depression after your grandfather's stroke. She also told me that your grandfather was a Holocaust survivor. I'm sure he must have talked about his experiences with you."

She sighed. "He would relive his memories over and over after he had his stroke. It was mainly because of him that I came to see Linda. It was so hard to listen to him and imagine the suffering he went through. It was even harder to realize what his life must have been like for so many years during the war. After he died I became very depressed."

Collin nodded. "Studies show only about 25% of Holocaust survivors ever recover from their trauma." Collin's voice was low, reverent. "The brain actually undergoes changes because of the enormous stress. Your grandfather was dealing with an overwhelming amount of grief, I'm sure."

"And guilt. He felt he had failed the prisoners in the camp where he'd been incarcerated. He thought he could've done more." Madison shook her head. "And then there was Edward."

Collin looked down at his notes. "Edward was your grandfather's older brother. It says here he was murdered by the Germans when your grandfather was a young teenager?"

Madison cleared her throat. "Edward was my grandfather's older brother... *and his hero.* After my grandfather had his stroke he talked about Edward all the time. Twenty seven priests were murdered that same day with Edward at the seminary near Gdansk in Northern Poland."

"Edward was a priest? So I take it your grandfather wasn't Jewish?"

"He was Catholic. Most people don't realize that close to three million Poles, who were not Jewish, the greatest number of them being Catholic gentiles, died in that country during the occupation by the Germans. Millions more were made slave laborers. There were also thousands of Catholic priests executed. That of course doesn't take into account the Polish Citizens who were killed or exiled by the Soviets to Siberia and died there."

Collin shook his head. "Sometimes I forget that not everyone who suffered and died during the Holocaust was Jewish."

Madison sighed. "It's been difficult educating people about that fact at times. Or the fact that the Soviets who were suppose to be Poland's allies secretly executed over twenty thousand elite officers in the Katyn forest. Almost everything that happened in Poland after the war was suppressed by the communist government that came to power. People in the U.S. usually hear only half of Poland's history and that's usually from Holocaust Centers that are run by Jewish Groups. There were other groups that the Nazis targeted besides Jews, gypsies and the disabled."

Collin nodded. "It was such a terrible time in history. So many people suffered. We're still learning more about the war every day."

Madison sat up straighter in her chair. "The really sad part of it all is that I've witnessed numerous times that Poles were actually blamed for the holocaust by misinformed people. In fact one of the biggest mistakes made in journalism around the globe is the use of the misleading term *Polish Concentration* Camp. The camps were located in Poland, but the German-Nazi's implemented them and incarcerated the Poles as well as the Jews. The risk of young people misunderstanding history and thinking the Poles ran the camps and collaborated with the Nazis is enormous when young people are just learning about history and only reading newspaper articles."

"I imagine it's very painful for a Polish survivor to see that mistake in a paper or on a website when they themselves suffered tremendously." Collin shook his head and looked down at his notes. "It says that you lost your father and mother when you were a young girl?"

"I was eleven years old when they died in a car accident. After they were both killed my grandfather and my aunt raised me."

"Wanda was your father's half sister? I read that she left the convent to get married."

"That's right." Madison felt herself grow unbearably warm. "What does this have to do my panic attack?"

"It helps to know your family history. One thing that stands out to me is that you are the granddaughter of a survivor. There's a definite pathology to children of survivors. They share their parent's and grandparent's memories. Often their own lives are greatly impacted by their family history."

"I can understand that." Madison frowned. "By the time I was sixteen I'd read every book on the Holocaust I could find to try to understand what my grandfather went through. There weren't many books about Polish Catholics then or even now. On memorials they usually fall under the category of "others," or non-Jews and people don't really recognize them." She took a breath. "Collin, I have great sympathy for everyone who was victimized during that time, Jews and Catholics alike. In fact, one of my favorite books is by a Jewish psychiatrist who was a prisoner in a concentration camp himself. The book changed my life. It helped me to understand how everything can be taken from you, but what matters most is your attitude." Madison looked down at her hands. "The war was so senseless and monstrous. The most horrifying thing of all was how many good people betrayed their own morals and that's what haunted my grandfather the most."

"It's called *Man's Search for Meaning*. Victor Frankel, a Jewish psychiatrist is the author. It's one of my favorites too." Collin rubbed his chin. "Did your grandfather ever talk to a professional?"

"If he had I'm unaware of it. I never realized how much of a problem it was for men to cry because I'd seen my grandfather cry so many times. I don't think a psychiatrist could have helped him because his pain was so deep."

"How did he deal with it?"

"Mainly he would do his artwork. He once told me that painting helped him take his sorrow and pain and create something beautiful out of them. He believed the only reason God had allowed him to survive the war was because he was suppose to fill the world with as much beauty as he could to counter the ugliness in human beings. My grandfather was an extraordinary artist himself. And such an inspiration to me," she added softly

"Your grandfather did what Frankel wrote about in his book.

He gave his suffering meaning."

Madison grabbed a tissue and dabbed at her eyes. "Before I met Nick, the meaning in my life *was* my grandfather. Collin. I remember lying in bed at night after hearing him cry in his bedroom when I was a little girl. I knew he was reliving something that happened during the war. It was heartbreaking. As a child I always wanted to comfort him, to make him stop crying." She paused and looked around the room. "The two men I loved the most in the world are gone now."

"What was your husband like Madison?"

Madison felt a lump growing in her throat. "Nick taught Special Needs students," she began. "His students and basically everyone who met him loved him. He claimed there were far more handicapped minds in some of the most intelligent people." She slowly raised her eyes to meet his and took a deep breath. "Sometimes I feel like my soul has died with my husband."

"I can assure you that you may have lost your husband, but definitely not your soul, Madison."

"What do you think is happening to me?"

"I know you're grieving. I also believe you're searching for the meaning in your husband's death. You may never get over losing your husband, but perhaps like your grandfather you can learn to temper your sorrow. I know you've been doing that already by working on your artwork. I've been to your gallery and have seen some of your paintings. They are extraordinary."

"Thank you," she said, feeling herself relax a little. His voice was calming. *Perhaps he wasn't the serial killer she thought him to be at one point and actually that angel Eden claimed he was.*

What do you think happened to me at the beach?"

Collin cleared his throat." Goliath was definitely acting very strange that day. At one point he actually growled at me in the water."

"How is he now?"

"I haven't noticed anything unusual in his behavior."

"What do you think he was barking at?"

"I've been meaning to go back to the beach and take another look, but I haven't had the chance. My first reaction was someone was in trouble. But if that were true, I'd hope Goliath would be in the water swimming out to save them and not standing on shore putting up a big fuss."

"Do you think the dog sensed something in the water was dangerous, perhaps a chemical?"

"That could be a possibility."

"My friend thought it was very possible that there was something toxic in the lake and your dog instinctively tried to warn us about it. Eden researches environmental toxins."

"Does she work for the DNR?"

"No actually she writes books for children. Eden belongs to the *Sacred Earth Society,* if you've ever heard of it."

"Is it an environmental group?"

` "*The Sacred Earth Society* is a group dedicated to promoting artists and writers who develop inspirational stories for children. Eden is a children's book author who is working on a series of books for children. The main character in one of them is a little Native American Girl named Minnie who is in tears all the time about what she sees happening to the earth because of man's carelessness. I was working on a painting for the cover of one of her books when I met you at the beach."

CHAPTER FOURTEEN

Collin took a sip of his coffee and flipped through his appointment book. Madison Andrews had agreed to bi-weekly visits, scheduling her appointments on Tuesdays and Thursdays. He was certain she was suffering from depression after the death of her husband.

He glanced around his office and shook his head. There was one small photograph of a maple tree with a white mat and a black frame hanging at eye level on one of the walls. He had taken the photograph in high school on his uncle's property of what he considered a perfect tree. *The family tree,* Devin always called it. He'd hoped to buy one of Madison's paintings to go along with it to compensate her for the mishap with Goliath at the beach. Unfortunately he'd had a tough time deciding on one after visiting her gallery. It was not astonishing considering the fact all of her art work had been extraordinary.

Collin leaned back in his chair and put his hands behind his head. He closed his eyes for a moment, then opened them again to stare at the small photo. He'd not been surprised at all to discover that Madison had been an art prodigy as a child after talking to her aunt at the gallery one day before he became her therapist. At the tender age of eight she'd been painting pictures that more experienced artists couldn't duplicate in style and technique. The word genius had come to his mind several times when he'd looked over the collection of oils that Madison had produced in the past several years before her husband's death. To say he'd been completely captivated was an understatement.

"Where she'd gotten the talent was everyone's question when they saw her art. I always knew it came from God so she could change the world," Wanda Kowalski had told him that afternoon.

After meeting with his last patient of the day, he decided to go home and take Goliath for a walk. When he returned from the park, he spent several minutes playing with the dog on the floor in the small living room, remembering the last time Devin had played with Goliath. Feeling loneliness creeping in, he found his cell phone and called Grosse Pointe hoping Jennifer would let him speak to his son for a few minutes without any deep discussions,.

When his ex-wife answered the phone, he tried not to wince at the sound of her voice. It sounded tense.

"Devin is away with the Boy Scouts. He'll be back on Sunday night," Jennifer said. "I'll have him call you then. So how is Traverse City?"

He realized she was making an extra effort to be cordial today.

"I find myself much more relaxed. I try not to read the newspapers if I can help it.

How's the weather been?"

"It's been pretty sensational, actually. I've been able to put in a few days of golf at Grand Traverse Resort."

"Sounds like you're doing OK."

"And you?" He could hear her take in a sharp breath.

"Oh you know me I'll survive, I'm a fighter."

"So what's going on Jennifer?"

"Nothing really, same old stuff." She paused. "I guess this gang thing is really getting to me. I know it's probably the only real sense of belonging many of those kids have, but I can't deal with it anymore. I can't deal with the language. My adrenaline takes a flying leap whenever I hear a profanity these days." She gave a tired laugh. "I lost it the other day, Collin. I told some poor kid in detention, and this was a girl mind you, that her filthy mouth was a disgrace and couldn't stand the crap that was spewing out of it. If we could get the language under control we could teach them, Collin, it's half the battle."

"Whew, talk about laying a guilt trip. Did you give the girl a detailed map?"

Jennifer was silent for several seconds. He could hear her breathing hard. He knew she was digesting his words, searching for the hidden meanings and accusations. The underlying layer of pain that accompanied each sentence they had spoken so far danced between them, stretching across the distance like an umbilical cord that he was afraid would always connect them to their failure.

"No, actually I told her she sounded like a little slut." Jennifer took another deep breath. "Good thing for a teacher to say, huh? And the girl's supposed to be emotionally impaired. I handled the situation with the sensitivity of a Mack track careening down a mountain with no brakes. I could have gotten fired. But these kids are driving me crazy. There are kids raising kids these days and it seems no one is paying attention and helping. We need to throw some money into programs for these children and not at the big corporations that are sucking up tax payer dollars. Besides that there are no role models for the kids, only reality shows." She finally gave a nervous laugh. "Alright there are millions of good people and role models. I just wish kids would pay attention to *them* more and not the air heads on television." She sighed. "Devin misses you a lot, Collin. When are you coming down to see him?"

He felt an onslaught of guilt hanging over him like an overhang of snow on a mountainside ready to chill his senses with the slightest careless move. "I'm hoping to get away by the end of next month. I hope I can take him out on the lake."

"He'd like that. I'm praying Metro Beach won't be closed again this summer because of the bacteria in the water. Well I should go, I have to get cleaned up, there's a meeting at school tonight."

With that Jennifer quickly hung up. For several moments afterwards, he sat on the sofa in his living room staring at his fish tank. He decided to take a nap. He was surprised when he woke up an hour later on the couch and realized he had dreamt of Madison Andrews. She had been standing on the beach near the lake, her long dark hair flowing down over her shoulders like a veil. A beam of brilliant white light held her captive while Goliath sat next to her. The dog's brown eyes had been glued to her adoringly.

Getting up from the couch he walked into his bedroom and changed into his jeans. Afterwards he headed out the door and drove to the beach where'd he 'd met her.

HE TOOK HIS TIME STROLLING ALONG the shore of Lake Michigan while Goliath meandered back and forth in front of him. He and the dog walked for about two miles until they came to an old tree stump. There Collin stopped to watch a freighter move along the horizon while he gathered his thoughts. The lake was calm and incredibly blue, like the sky overhead; it reminded him of Madison's eyes.

The memory of Madison standing in the lake with water up to her waist and filled with fright made him feel disoriented somehow. She'd reminded him of the doe he'd come across caught in a barbwire fence near his uncle's estate when he was a kid. There was no way he'd ever forget the fear in that animal's eyes. When he and his dad had finally gotten close to her, and were working to set the beautiful creature free, the feel of her shaking limbs in his hands and the fear that had vibrated throughout her body had left an impression on him so deep that it had lasted throughout his life. He would always remember that precise moment when the doe had hurriedly leapt away only to stop for a moment and gaze back at them as though amazed a man could come so close and not harm her. He had committed his life to setting things free that day. It tore him up inside to see people *and animals* treated as if they had no feelings and felt no pain. He knew he would starve if he ever had to hunt for food.

But at that precise moment he also knew he had the tough task of setting himself free. He was all too aware of the fact he and Jennifer had created a son together. He was filled with a great deal of his own fear that his son would become one of the statistics, one of the children whose psyches were forever impacted by their parent's mistakes. Many times in the darkness of his bedroom on the threshold of a fitful sleep he'd apologized to Devin for the turmoil in his young life.

COLLIN HAD NO IDEA HOW LONG HE'D STOOD on the beach lost in his thoughts. He was only sure he'd come to the place Goliath had stood barking and where he'd set Madison down when he carried her back to shore that first day he met her. It was when a seagull shrieked overhead that he looked around and realized the dog had wandered off again. It was at that instant that something caught his eye in the water. It had only been a second just long enough to register on his brain and kick in his adrenaline.

He remembered a patient he'd treated when he first started his practice. The woman claimed her daughter and she had not bonded because of PBB's that had been accidentally dumped into cattle feed. She'd been nursing her newborn at the time only to discover that a fire retardant had been accidentally fed to a herd of dairy cows and was in the food chain. The possibility that the contamination was showing up in human breast milk was a real possibility. As a young mother, the woman had spent a number of anxiety filled weeks getting advice from everyone on what to do. She finally decided to quit breast feeding only to develop an all encompassing fear as her daughter was growing up that the girl was in constant danger. The woman's over protective stance had destroyed their mother-daughter relationship at one point.

He had learned in his practice not to take anything lightly and if there was the slightest possibility there was a problem with some sort of toxin in the lake, he knew he would not feel comfortable ignoring it.

CHAPTER FIFTEEN

When Madison finally glanced at Collin again, he was looking down at the notebook on his desk. "I took a year off after art school, before I met Nick," she began, glancing at the picture of the maple tree hanging on the wall in his office. "I traveled Europe. I visited Paris and saw the Louvre. I visited Rome and the Vatican. I pinched myself the day I stood gazing up at the Sistine Chapel. I was in awe of its beauty. Afterwards I walked the Apian Way and wound up at the little church of Quo Vadis during my hike around Rome. I'd remembered my grandfather talking about the chapel. He told me he made a pilgrimage there after the war. Many believed it was where Jesus appeared to St. Peter, when he was fleeing Rome when Nero set it on fire. I said several prayers when I got there. The words stuck in my throat at one point, because I was so mad at God for what happened to my parents and family. But I desperately needed to believe he was listening."

She glanced around the office then looked down at her hands for a moment before she continued. "When I got to Berlin I stood on a street corner and pictured Nazi soldiers marching in the streets. I remember being so angry that afternoon knowing what happened to my grandfather and his family in Poland. I was so angry I wanted to break windows. But I got over it soon enough after meeting an old German woman in a deli there. She had the most haunting blue eyes I'd ever seen. On a whim, I asked if I could sketch her. I was surprised that she said yes."

Madison took a deep breath and shifted position in her seat. "The woman's face was creviced and lined, Collin. She was very old, but there was a dignity in her that was so beautiful. I have always loved doing drawings of women of all ages, especially older women, you can see the story of their lives etched into their expressions, you can see their laughter and their tears."

She took another deep breath and shook her head. "While I was sketching this German woman, who owned the deli with her daughter, she told me her story. It was surprising they knew English so well." Madison paused and looked down at her hands. "That day changed my life forever. Why she related so much of her life to me is a mystery. It was just so personal. I always believed I was suppose to be there that day, to hear her story. because I needed to know."

"How did it change your life?"

"Before that I hated Germans. Hitler had caused so much pain, death and destruction. And no one in that country stopped him."

" Do you still hate them?"

"Collin I can't hate anyone, now. I just hate war. I've learned that everyone suffers."

"What did she tell you?"

"She told me about her sister and what happened when the Soviet soldiers entered the city after the destruction of Berlin." Madison paused and looked away. She finally met his eyes squarely. "Apparently her sister was one of thousands of German women who were gang raped by the soldiers when they took over. She herself, managed to hide, but her older sister wasn't so lucky."

Collin let out a breath. "I've read something about it. Unfortunately the Soviets did what many advancing armies have done throughout the ages."

"The abuse was horrific, she told me very young girls as young as eight and even very old women were raped over and over by gangs of soldiers as the army advanced. Every woman in their path was abused whatever age they were or whether they were pregnant. It was so horrible. After the war none of the women talked about it. They lived their lives in such darkness and severe depression if they managed to survive. They also lived with horrible shame. She said that it was sadly the way of the world, that women should be punished for what the men did, for the wars they created with each other. She said the women had no power to control or stop anything. They had been at the mercy of the Nazis and of course always the men."

"Wasn't she angry about it? What happened to her sister? Is she still alive?"

. "She told me many women took their own lives afterwards. They just couldn't go on with the horrible memories." Madison paused. "It was several years after the war when her sister fixed dinner for what was left of her family that she slipped into her bedroom afterwards, and shot herself."

Madison took a deep breath and shook her head. Tears sprang to her eyes. "I found out doing my research just how horrible the abuse of women was throughout Europe during the war. To me the assaults were war crimes. These women were not soldiers, they were civilians caught up in the madness. But of course many of the assaults were never reported, the world felt they had it coming, I guess because they were German. Besides that the women were too traumatized and too ashamed. It was worse than death for many of them."

Collin nodded. "Sadly it is only now people are coming forward and these stories are being told."

Madison shook her head. "I began to study the holocaust because I wanted to know the truth about what happened to my grandfather. I got much more than I anticipated." She retrieved a tissue from the box next her and wiped her eyes. "I paint to fill my mind with beauty. It's my shield against all the ugliness I run across. Painting is my voice a voice that so many unfortunate women in this world don't have."

"Your artwork is beautiful, Madison. When did you start painting?"

She glanced up at the ceiling for a moment. "Since I was very young. The artwork really started because of my grandfather. He was quite the artist. He experimented in all kinds of mediums; pastels and oil, even woodworking. I remember he actually built a lathe so he could experiment with it. He tooled a goblet out of pine on the lathe for me when I was a little girl. I was in Catholic school at the time and thought of it as a chalice. At that young age I actually wanted to be a priest until I found out girls couldn't be priests. I don't know what happened to it. I look back on it all now and cherish that memory of my grandfather in his workroom when he handed me this cup, like he was passing down something to me as a child, something that was very special and mysterious and very holy". She shook her head. "He was such a good person. If you knew him you would have loved him too."

She grabbed another tissue out of the box next to her and finally looked at him. "I began to heal when I made my way to Poland, I had never been there, but it felt like I had gone home." She gave him a small smile. "It's not what I expected or imagined."

"What did you imagine?"

"A very dark place, filled with poor illiterate peasants like the media depicts. I imagined so much less than it actually is. At one time it was the biggest country in Europe where Jewish people from around the world settled because of it's tolerance to other faiths. There were no persecutions in the country similar to the Inquisitions in Spain. There were different faiths living side by side, including Muslims. Poland is filled with wonderful architecture and beautiful scenery. There are museums everywhere. There are beautiful palaces and castles throughout the country that you can actually stay in. There are also beautiful parks in all the towns and cities. I think the resort town of Zakopane is my favorite place. The Tatra Mountains are absolutely breathtaking. I was told that the Pope went skiing there and loved the town. I can see why. The whole area is stunning."

Collin nodded. "I remember reading that Hitler didn't have the city of Krakow bombed because it was so beautiful."

"Yes, I've heard that too. My grandfather loved Krakow and had gone to school at the Jagellion University for a couple of years. Krakow was actually called the Paris of the East. And I can see why. Cloth Hall is stunning. Rynek square is amazing. It's the biggest town center in all of Europe. It's on a scale as grand as anything I've seen in Paris or London." She cleared her throat. "I sat under the statue of the *Poet*, Adam Mickiewicz, in Rynek Square and did some art work one day. I watched the children and the lovers holding hands and strolling along. It was hard to imagine all that transpired there at one time. It's hard to imagine the people there coped with so much brutality, but still had the will to rebuild and become their own country again after so many years of occupation."

"It sounds like the trip made a huge impact on you, Madison."

"Yes, it did in many ways. It was something I had to do to understand my heritage." She sighed. "To me Poland is a very special place, but special in a unique way, because it's where the very worst and the very best of humanity existed side by side. Only so much of the time we don't hear enough about the best, we always hear about the worst." She took a deep breath. "I have viewed videos blaming the Poles for erecting the concentration camps, instead of the German Nazis. I've run across articles that claimed that so many Jewish people died in Poland because of the anti-semitic Catholics there and not because the country was taken over by the Germans who put the entire country under siege and occupation. The Gestapo threatened to kill anyone, including their families if they helped Jewish people in any way." She paused. "The fact that three million gentiles who were mostly Catholics were also murdered and led to concentration camps seems to be lost on many people. And they don't realize that millions of Polish gentiles were slave laborers and were slated to be worked to death by the Nazis. Add to that close to a million and a half people that were sent to Siberia by the Soviets. I'm sorry, I'm talking so much about this, Collin. The whole thing makes me very passionate, because it's very personal for me. My grandfather was one of those people."

"I commend you for what you've tried to do, Madison. And what you are doing now. I don't think I could face so much. You are very courageous." Collin finally gave her a small smile. "I hope you don't mind if I change the subject, but you mentioned you went back to the lake. How are you feeling now about what happened there?"

"I think I'm dealing with it much better than I was at first. I'm sure I had a panic attack because of Goliath. I was always a little frightened of very large dogs when I was a child."

"Did you do any of your artwork?" he finally asked looking up at her and giving her a smile.

"I worked on a picture of a schooner."

"A schooner? Will you do a painting?"

"I'm not sure. I just had the urge to sketch one. I did wade out into the lake again that afternoon to take a look at the wreckage we came across. Afterwards I happened to talk to one of the curators at the nautical museum in town. He told me he believed what we saw and what Goliath was barking at was wreckage from the Lydia B, a small nineteenth century schooner that used to travel back and forth from Chicago. There really wasn't much to it. It was a tangle of wooden beams and seaweed. I also saw some canisters that were caught in the middle of the wreckage. Most of all it smelled like rotting fish. It wasn't what I expected."

"I also talked to the curator several weeks ago," Collin looked down at his notes. "There's a very interesting story behind the shipwreck. Did you see the article that was hanging on the wall in the museum?

"Yes, I told my aunt Wanda about it."

Does your aunt know what happened at the beach before I took you to the hospital that day?

"She's been very worried about me since it happened. Maybe this sounds rather silly, but I feel I've let her down."

"What do you mean?"

"Wanda has always been terrified something bad was going to happen to me. She's been like that since I was a little girl. I really do understand it, especially after what happened to my parents in the car accident." She paused. "Lately she's been having some dreams that have been very disturbing. Something bad happened to her in Poland. She's never told me exactly what it was."

"I hope you won't add to your problems by feeling guilty about something you had no control over. Are there other things you feel guilty about?"

"In what way?"

"I think you feel guilty because you couldn't help your grandfather. I imagine you as a young girl trying to deal with his past and being unable in any way to relieve the heartache for him. That in itself sets you up for a good amount of guilt and despair."

"I did try so hard to make my grandfather happy. I guess there were many times I'd felt I'd failed him."

"Tell me how you failed him?"

"I always tried to tell his story. I wanted people to understand that the history that they were taught in school is far more complicated than they were led to believe. It broke my heart to see how people misunderstood my grandfather at times and how I couldn't make them understand his pain."

"Madison I do think you've put yourself under an awful lot of pressure throughout your life," he said gently. We haven't talked about your husband's death as much as your grandfather's. I get the impression you feel an enormous amount of guilt there also. There's a lot going on inside of you emotionally."

"Nick is dead, Collin. My guilt or anybody else's won't bring him back." She reached for a Kleenex and wiped her eyes.

"I'm sure you did all you could for Nick when he was ill, but I believe deep inside you haven't convinced yourself of it."

"You don't know what it was like." She shuddered. "Nick was so full of life."

His voice was gentle. "And in your eyes Nick was perfect."

"What do you mean?"

"I think you put Nick on a pedestal. But Nick was subject to all the maladies life dishes out. I think you're angry because you feel in your heart he let you down by dying and leaving you."

"Linda also pointed out the fact I was angry. Have you concluded that's the reason for my blackout?"

"The human mind is complex. I can't help but think somewhere inside of you a piece of your life has shifted. It's causing other pieces to move out of place, so to speak, and to hit some invisible switch in your head at times. Are your doctors going to run any more tests?"

"They've done all the tests they can for now. I can't help thinking about how Nick died."

"Are you afraid something like that is going to happen to you?"

"Nick didn't drink or smoke. He took care of himself. One day while we were running together, he collapsed. The next day they found a malignant tumor the size of a tennis ball next to his heart. Eventually the cancer worked its way into his brain."

"You told me the doctors haven't found anything unusual with your tests."

"I can't help but wonder about what caused Nick's cancer? They warn you not to eat too much of the fish caught in Lake

Michigan because of the mercury."

"Do you think you may've been exposed to the same thing that caused your husband's cancer?"

"I've heard of people who were exposed to chemicals that had symptoms similar to mine."

"What about the blackout?"

She took a deep breath. "It's frightening to think I can't remember anything that happened after I stepped into the water."

CHAPTER SIXTEEN

The oil painting that he'd purchased at the Northern Cross, several days before, sat on the floor of his office leaning against the wall. Collin took a sip of his coffee and studied the canvas. The sunset over the beach, near the lighthouse Madison had painted, was absolutely breathtaking. He'd hoped to surprise her with it hanging on the wall, when she came in for her therapy session, but unfortunately she hadn't shown up nor had he been able to hang it. It was the first time she'd missed an appointment in the six weeks since she'd started seeing him.

He glanced at the appointment book in front of him. An hour ago he'd directed his receptionist to leave a message at the gallery about the missed session. He was hopeful Madison would call. She'd told him, when he last saw her, that she was feeling somewhat better, but he had a hunch it was like her to say she was doing better than she actually was.

His receptionist paged him to pick up the phone. Wanda Kowalski's voice was hoarse and raspy. "Two fishermen found her lying on the beach yesterday morning. She was unconscious!" Wanda paused to take a breath. "They saw Madison from their boat when they were making their way into the harbor to escape the storm. I am so thankful they found her before anything bad happened. I will keep you posted about her condition. She's in the hospital again!"

"Thank you, Wanda, I'd really appreciate it if you kept me updated." Collin let out his own breath and glanced at Madison's painting. *Another episode at the beach!* He knew Madison believed and had been comforted by the idea that she'd had a panic attack because of Goliath. How would she feel knowing there was no dog to blame this incident on?

He spent the rest of the day feeling anxious, forgetting an appointment he'd scheduled at noon. At lunch he overheard a man in the small deli in town mention a woman who'd been found on the beach unconscious the day before. He knew the man had been referring to Madison. Collin ate his sandwich, not really tasting it, and quickly returned to his office only to find another patient he'd forgotten waiting for him. He realized as he hurried into the room he was anxious to see Madison for himself and know she was alright. Her aunt had mentioned she'd be released in a day or two.

EDEN'S FACE WAS SET in a frown as she hovered over Madison with a small bouquet of flowers. "How are you feeling?" she asked.

Madison sat up a little straighter in the bed. She gave Eden a thin smile. "The doctor said I'd be going home tomorrow. Apparently, once again, they have no idea why this is happening to me. She finally winced and looked down at her arm. "The purple bruises on my arm are fading, thank goodness. I think they've taken enough blood to keep the Red Cross in business for another year."

Eden gave her a peck on the cheek. She slipped the bouquet of pink roses she'd been holding into a vase near the bed. "Promise me you won't decide to add any more excitement to my mundane existence. I felt the baby do a back flip when Wanda told me what happened to you! I was so worried!"

"I'm sorry about all of this, Eden, but I think I may be going off the deep end."

"Madison you need to take care of yourself. I don't think you're eating enough."

"That's what my aunt said."

"How's Wanda holding up?"

"She's pretty shaken. That can be expected. I think she's holding up pretty well though considering the fact I feel I've let her down."

"What do you mean?"

"Wanda has been adamant for the past several weeks that something was going to happen to me. I kept telling her not to worry. I guess this has proved her right."

"Well tell her it's all over. Tell her she doesn't have to worry anymore because everything that could possibly happen to you in one lifetime has happened."

'Try convincing my aunt of that. From now on I know she'll be hovering over me like I'm a child.

Eden pulled a chair over to the side of the bed and sat down. "Is she still having those strange dreams?"

"Unfortunately that's the reason this is so upsetting to her." Madison frowned. "She believes the young woman who she dreamt about was the one who was killed near Detroit several weeks ago. She's worried that I'm in some sort of danger too."

"Has she dreamt of you?'

"I have a feeling she has."

"Do you think your aunt is suffering from post traumatic stress like your grandfather was?"

"She's been carrying around an enormous amount of guilt for something that happened in the past that she had no control over. Only she won't tell me exactly what it was."

Eden shook her head. "What were you doing before you fainted? Do you remember anything at all?"

"I remember wading into the lake."

"Why did you go into the water?"

"Remember when I told you about the dog barking at the water? It turns out there's wreckage from a small ship near the shore. It sank in the early 1800's. I talked to the curator at the nautical museum in town that morning. They knew about the schooner. It's been moved about along the shoreline because of the storms we've been having. There was an article on the wall of the museum about the ship. Apparently there was a mysterious death on board the vessel."

"Maybe the person who died is haunting you and that's why you're having these problems." Eden gave a soft laugh.

Madison sighed. "I wish it were that simple. When the doctors were taking all those tests, I actually wished they'd find something wrong with me so I'd know what I'm dealing with. What will I do if this happens again?"

CHAPTER SEVENTEEN

Madison flipped through the spiral sketch book to see if any of the pictures had been damaged. Apparently someone had dropped the book off at the gallery before she'd been released from the hospital. She'd picked it up several days ago and had left it in her car. It was a miracle it was still intact. She stopped abruptly. Her mouth hung open in surprise. On top of the sketch of the schooner she'd been working on at the beach there was something written in pencil.

> *I see you crying,*
> *I wonder how my touch,*
> *Can soothe your heart*
> *White shows so much*
> *Against dark*

It looked like her handwriting. It also looked like some kind of poem. She studied the rest of the sketches, scouring each page for anything unusual. When she came to the back of the book, she once again halted in surprise. *How was it possible that she didn't remember drawing it?*

The man in the sketch had large eyes and dark hair with long sideburns. It definitely was her work. It matched perfectly her style and the technique she used for pencil portraits.

She quickly stuffed the book into her canvas bag and opened the door of her car. Bewildered, she walked up the driveway to the outside stairway to the second floor of the Victorian.

Eden was certain grief was causing the memory problems. Eden had brought her several articles to read while she'd been in the hospital. The one that stood out to her was written by a mother whose daughter had died on a plane sabotaged by a terrorist. The mother's anger at the loss of her daughter had made her bitter at a world she felt didn't understand the intense pain of dealing with her a tragedy like hers. In some ways she could identify with the mother. She realized she'd been struggling to have her feelings go away like some rare disease. Perhaps it was the struggle itself that was causing her problems.

She headed up to her apartment to change. She had promised Eden that she would meet her at the Crooked Tree restaurant for dinner at six. From there Eden had suggested they go to Belles Tavern just south of Traverse City where they could enjoy some music. She hadn't been to Belles in over three years. It was where she had first heard Nick play with his band.

EDEN WAS SITTING AT A TABLE near one of the windows with a view of the lake when Madison arrived at the restaurant. Madison looked around the large dining room filled to overflowing with people. She knew there had been a steady stream of tourists visiting Eagle Bay from around the country since the television show *Good Morning America* had aired about Sleeping Bear Dunes National Lakeshore.

"You look nice, Madison," Eden exclaimed. She took her purse off the table and set it down on the chair next to her.

Madison slipped into a seat by the window. "So do you. I like your new haircut. It looks like you put more highlights in your hair too. Have I kept you waiting?"

"Not long.. I'm just so glad you decided to go tonight."

"I wasn't planning on it, but I am feeling a bit better." She finally looked out the window for several moments.

"What's wrong? You look so anxious. Are you sure you're feeling better?"

She shook her head. "I found some things in my sketch book

that are bothering me."

"What kind of things?"

"I drew a picture of a man. There was also some writing on one of the pages. It sounds like some sort of poem. I really don't remember putting them there."

Just then a waitress came up to their table. "What can I get you to drink?" she asked, handing them menus.

Eden glanced down at her stomach. "I think I'll just have water."

After ordering a glass of wine, Madison gazed out the window at the procession of boats going past the restaurant. Two sailboats with brightly colored sails were making their way to the lake. Nick had always wanted a sailboat. Her throat grew tight. She had planned on buying him one as a surprise after he finished his last round of chemo.

"I think we should take a peek at the menu sometime soon, Madison." Eden whispered.

"I'm sorry, I was just thinking."

"Hopefully you'll be able to enjoy yourself tonight. And not think too much! I've heard some very good reviews on the band that's playing at Belles tonight."

"Nick played there several times."

Eden gave her a sad smile. "Nick had an awesome voice. I will always remember those times his band put on something for the Special Ed students. Nick was such a great guy. Every one of those kids loved him." Eden shook her head. "It was such fun going to the charity events at their school." Eden's face suddenly grew pale. "Madison, I want you to keep calm, but it appears Vincent Strickland has just walked in with a date." She motioned to the front of the restaurant.

Madison glanced in the direction of the main door. Vincent was standing at the hostess station with a woman with short dark hair who looked to be at least a decade older than him. She let out a breath when she realized the hostess was escorting them to the a table at the far end of the dining room.

"Are you going to say something about the paintings?"

Madison shook her head. "Not here. I think I need to take care of it in my own way."

Eden sighed. "I think you're in denial, Madison. I'm

extremely worried about you."

"Eden, please, I really can't talk about this right now."

Eden nodded. "Alright I'll change the subject, but just for the moment, if you promise me you'll talk to someone about Vincent. *And be very careful!*" Eden finally picked up her glass and took a drink of her water. "By the way, did I mention that mom is in the process of cleaning out the attic? "She's stored this enormous oil painting of my great grandfather up there for decades. I remember she had it removed from the dining room when I was a kid, because it terrified me. I guess I told her the eyes in the picture looked alive and were following me wherever I went. You know how kids are." Eden gave a small laugh."

"I feel like there are eyes watching me at this very moment."

Eden turned her head slightly. He's busy talking to his girl friend right now." She glanced back at Madison and continued her story. "The portrait's been in the attic for many years. From what I've heard about my great grandfather, he used to be quite a player, or as mom put it, a lady's man."

"When was it painted?"

In the late 1800's. It was before the fire of course."

"Are there any portraits of your great grandmother?"

"There are numerous old photographs of Lydia. I haven't come across any paintings that were done of her. She was very modest. I think she was pretty, but definitely not in Nathanial's class of looks. I know that's a strange thing to say about your great grandfather, but it's true. Apparently Lydia inherited a great deal of money just before she married my great grandfather. This restaurant actually sits on the old site where the resort hotel she built used to be."

"She actually built a hotel?"

"Wealthy people from Chicago used to vacation in this area. Eagle Bay was quite a spot for tourists in it's hey day. Sadly most of the old resorts in town burnt in the fire."

"I wonder who the young woman was who planted the rose hedge. I keep thinking about her."

"It would be interesting to find out. We should ask Margaret if we can see the journals. They have a library of old diaries at the historical society kept by important people from the town. Maybe we can find an interesting plot to develop around the poem you wrote."

Madison winced. "What was the name of the man who was apparently psychic and diagnosed people's illnesses in his sleep? Who knows, maybe I'll write a best selling novel the next time I pass out."

Eden shook her head. "I don't like the thought of you being *out of it,* Madison. Promise me you've had the last of these episodes so we can both get on with life without any more worries. Can I ask you something? How's your therapy going? Is it helping at all?"

"It helps to talk to someone."

"You don't sound too enthusiastic. "Do you like Collin?"

"I do. I know he cares about his patients."

"I saw him at the gallery one day when you were in the hospital. He was talking to Wanda. You do know he's divorced, right?"

Madison felt her face grow warm.

"You like him a lot, don't you?"

"I told you I did."

"I don't mean as a therapist."

"Eden, please!"

"When is Dr. Bishop coming back from Florida?"

"Why?"

"Collin won't be your therapist then. You told me he asked you out to lunch."

"That was before he knew he would be treating me. What are you getting at?"

"Madison, "I want you to be happy. Nick would want you to be happy."

"I don't need another man in my life."

"Someday you will."

They finished their meals in silence. Finally Madison reached for her purse. "I need to go up front to the office and talk to Jessica for a moment. She's going to cater an event at the gallery for me. I'll be right back."

She slipped out of her chair and headed towards the front of the restaurant. She had to nudge her way around several couples to get to the office. When she finally came out of the office, she spotted Vincent standing at the hostess desk talking to one of the waitresses. She had to walk past him to get back to the table! Her heart picked up speed.

"Hello Madison," he said.

She nodded, "Hello, Vincent." She hoped she could get around him without another word, but her path was blocked by a couple waiting for their table. "Excuse me," she whispered to the middle aged woman in front of her. The woman stepped to the side, leaving a space. When Madison attempted to squeeze past her, Vincent caught her arm and held it.

"It's nice seeing you," he said, as their eyes met.

She felt his hand closing tighter and tighter around her arm. She tried to pull away. "Vincent, please you're hurting me."

"Madison, why did you make me believe you loved me?"

Just at that moment, Vincent's date emerged from the bathroom that was near the entrance. "I think I left my sunglasses on the table, Vincent," she said coming up behind Madison.

Vincent let go of her arm. Madison made her way to the back of the restaurant and her table. She slipped into her chair trying to catch her breath.

Eden stared at her for several moments. "You look like you've seen a ghost! You must have talked to Vincent. What did he say?"

"I really didn't give him a chance to say anything about the paintings. When I tried to get by him he grabbed my arm. His date came up from behind and he let go of me then."

"Madison, we need to at least say something to his girlfriend. I'd hate to have her find out about Vincent the hard way!"

CHAPTER EIGHTEEN

Eden held up her glass. "I'm relegated to sipping Cokes until the baby is born," she exclaimed. "Here's to a fun night. And here's to my friend, Madison. One of the best friends a girl could have in the world!"

Madison held up her own glass. "That goes for you too, darling." She gave Eden a tired smile and took a sip of her drink. Afterwards she looked around the large main room. Belles Tavern was an eclectic mix. Antiques hung from the walls and ceilings along with old photographs and paintings in a stunning montage of color and design. She realized the booth they were sitting in was made out of mahogany from an old sailboat.

"This place is very impressive." Eden looked up at the ceiling. "I heard they're still renovating. I'm just trying to figure out how they managed to get that old player piano up there. I do believe Margaret Wickers would love it here."

"How are the plans going for the museum benefit?"

"They decided that the tables will be set up on the lawn under canopies for the dinner. Several musicians are scheduled to play old fashioned instruments like dulcimers. They also are going to have a number of demonstrations, wood carving and quilt making, to name a few."

"I feel guilty that I haven't gotten the sketches together for you sooner. I'll try to get the pictures I have of the old church matted so we can set up some kind of display."

"I'm going to ask Margaret to bring some of the diaries we've talked about."

"How about the picture of Nathanial?"

"That might not be a bad idea. Mom could find some of her old photographs of Lydia too."

"I remember you telling me that your great grandfather had a bit of a reputation?" Madison made a face. She suddenly felt a bit tipsy and gave Eden a lopsided smile. She hadn't eaten much for dinner at the Crooked Tree.

"He apparently loved the ladies."

"I wonder how your great grandmother dealt with it.'

"It appears she kept herself busy. Apparently she thought it was more fun building hotels than anything women did back then.."

Just then a couple of musicians appeared on stage and the crowd began to applaud and whistle.

"They play a mixture of contemporary music and old rock." Eden said, looking up at the stage.

Madison heard several loud whistles coming from the booth behind her. She took another sip of her drink and looked over the crowd.

"I think you'll enjoy the band"

Madison nodded again and glanced up to watch one of the band members appear from a door beside the stage. He reminded her of Nick. Five minutes later, the rest of the band appeared. Tears came to her eyes. She made a face.

"What's the matter?"

Madison shook her head. There were couples everywhere holding hands, scooting their chairs around the tables to sit next to each other so they could touch while enjoying the music

Eden leaned towards a little to speak above the noise. "I can tell you're thinking too much, Madison!"

"It's hard not to."

"Maybe you should have another rum and coke!"

They sat through several songs watching a number of couples near them leave their chairs and head to the dance floor. The men and women wrapped their arms around each other and swayed with the music.

Madison gestured towards the front of the building. "I'm going to the restroom."

"Do you think you need a body guard?"

Madison shook her head. "Only if Vincent and his girlfriend show up."

She made her way through the maze of mismatched tables and chairs and a number of assorted antiques. Taking her place at the end of a line long line that ended near the men's bathroom, she studied the gallery of old photographs on the wall.

"Madison?"

She turned to see who had spoken.

Collin gave her a smile. "It's good to see you out enjoying yourself. Who are you here with?"

She suddenly felt flushed. "A friend of mine," she replied suddenly feeling flushed. She glanced around the tavern unable to meet his eyes. "

"A friend?"

"My friend, Eden. Have you been here before?"

"No this is the first time," Collin said, leaning up against an old telephone booth that was painted bright red and was made into an aquarium.

"My husband used to play here with his band." Nervously she brushed her hair away from her face. "So tell me, did you bring a date?" She wondered what the woman looked like.

"No, actually I brought Jim. I guess you could consider him my date. He's not as attractive as I would have liked." Collin gave her a small laugh then grew serious. "His wife died last year too. So where are you sitting?" he asked, quickly changing the subject.

She could smell his cologne. The masculine fragrance had always been one of her favorites. "We're sitting in one of the booths with an old player piano hanging over us," she said, feeling a bit giddy.

Collin ran his fingers through his sandy brown hair, combing it back with his fingers. "That sounds dangerous."

"She had to admit he looked great. He was wearing a loosely fitting white shirt tucked into a pair of jeans. He looked casual but elegant. Several women in front of her were staring at him."

The line was moving faster now and she took several steps to catch up with the lady in front of her. "See you later," she said glancing back at him. With a feeling of disappointment she watched him stroll into the great room and disappear into the crowd.

When she got back to her table the band was taking a short break. She found Eden talking to their waitress.

"I ordered another drink."

"For?"

"You're not driving. Why not enjoy?"

"I just saw Collin," she said glancing around the room again. He's here with a friend of his, someone by the name of Jim."

"It's destiny!"

"He's my therapist, Eden."

"What's that old expression? All's fair in love and war."

Madison sighed. "Life is not always fair."

"You'll feel better after you have another drink!" Eden twisted in her seat to see the bar. Our waitress is probably in the kitchen somewhere tearing her hair out. Look at all these people!"

When the band started playing again, Madison found herself searching the tables near the dance floor for Collin. She could see several young women sitting near the front. There were two middle aged couples sipping their drinks and a number of empty tables with half full glasses on them."

"Are you looking for him?"

Quickly she shook her head. Grabbing her glass, she slid an ice cube into her mouth. Just as she put the glass down she spotted Collin. The lady he was dancing with was very pretty. When the song was finished, she watched his hand linger on the woman's shoulder for a few moments before he returned to his own seat.

Eden tapped her arm to get her attention. "Want to dance?"

Madison hesitated, finally she nodded. *"Am I actually feeling jealous?"*

They waited for a fast song. When an old classic, *Proud Mary* began to play Eden motioned her to the dance floor. She caught a glimpse of Collin from where they stood. She realized he was watching her dance. The second song was one of her favorites, *Lady by Little River Band.* Looking around the tavern she noticed a few other single women dancing together. She glanced over at Collin's table again. He smiled at her when she caught his eye.

When they finally sat down, Eden's face was flushed. "I think the baby got a good workout. I know I felt it kick! I think she liked the music," Eden swiped at her forehead and let out a breath. She took a long sip of her drink as she settled back in her chair to watch the crowd. Five minutes later she was tugging on Madison's arm again. "Come on, let's go!"

Once more they made their way to the front of the tavern. Madison glanced at the table where she last saw Collin sitting. It was empty. Her eyes swept the room.

Eden threw her arms up in the air and waved them around. "I love this song!" It was only seconds later that she was lying on her back on the floor.

Madison gasped and dropped down on her knees beside her. She put her ear to Eden's mouth and checked her breathing.

Eden's eyes fluttered open for a moment. "What happened?"

Madison shook her head. "If this is one of your newest dance moves, I think you better find a new partner. You're scaring the daylights out of me. "

Eden gave a weak laugh. "Ha, ha," she whispered, her voice trailing off as she closed her eyes again.

It took ten minutes before the ambulance arrived. Madison finally let go of Eden's hand when one of the paramedics motioned everyone to move back. She watched anxiously as they lifted Eden onto a stretcher and wheeled her towards the door of the tavern.

Collin walked up and put his hand on her shoulder. "Are you okay?"

She turned to meet his eyes. "Eden's pregnant, Collin."

Collin studied her face. "Let's wait and see, before you get too worried,"

She nodded and tried to smile, suddenly growing dizzy. She made a face.

Collin gestured to the door. "Let me drive you to the hospital. You don't look too well yourself."

"I'd appreciate it. My car isn't here. Eden drove. I hate to see you stuck at the hospital again."

"I think I'll survive another trip." He took her elbow and guided her through the building. His friend Jim, was waiting by the front door.

"I'm going to the hospital with Madison.. I think she could use the company," Collin said to his friend. "Madison, this is Jim.

Most people call him Dr. Thompson."

Jim gave her a reassuring smile. "Odds are your friend will be just fine. If you have any problems, feel free to take two aspirin, but please don't call me because I'm only an eye doctor." He gave her a wink.

A moment later, Collin guided her through the entrance and across the parking lot to his vehicle. He helped her in and shut the door.

She leaned back against the leather seat. With a sigh she closed her eyes. Collin put his hand on her arm. "Madison? Are you sure you're okay?"

She took a deep breath. "It's been a rather exciting evening."

"Jim told me Belles was where it was all happening," He gave her a smile. "Apparently Jim was right."

"Jim seems like a very nice man," she said, glancing out the window at the trees in front of the tavern that were decorated with blue lights.

"He's been rather lonely since Julie died." Collin quickly changed the subject. "You're a good dancer," he said as he started the engine."

"So are you. Have you been to any of the night clubs in Traverse City yet?"

"No, this is my first big adventure out since I moved up here. Actually I'm a homebody." He pulled the SUV onto the road.

"It's hard to tell by the way you danced."

Collin chuckled softly. "I guess my old bones still have some rhythm."

She could tell he was still smiling a moment later and envisioned him the first day they had met on the beach. He was definitely a very striking man with his wavy sun bleached brown hair and dark sleepy brown eyes. She wondered if he'd gotten the phone number of the woman he'd danced with him. If not, she was sure the lady had been very disappointed.

"How's Goliath? she finally asked.

"He'll survive. As long as there's food around Goliath is a happy camper. I know he misses Devin."

They drove on in silence for another quarter of a mile while she gazed at the silhouettes of trees alongside the road.

"It's strange what's happened tonight," she finally whispered.

He turned his head slightly towards her.

"One week ago I was in the hospital, now Eden is ill."

"Do you think there's a connection? Or are you connecting things because the human mind needs order and some explanation?"

"I guess I need to know what's happening to me, to both Eden and myself." She became quiet again, as she watched the white line in the road. The highway was deserted. It reminded her of the night she'd pulled over in the rain near the lighthouse. She wondered if they'd ever found the woman who'd wandered from the group home. She hadn't heard anything about her since then.

Collin held his hand near the radio. "Would you like me to turn it on?"

"Actually I like the silence," she said watching his fingers hover near the buttons.

"So do I. Sometimes it just gets too quiet for me without Devin around."

She wanted to tell him that she knew how he felt, that her life was much too empty now without Nick, but she stared at the road guessing he didn't need to hear any more sad stories from her, not here and not now. She felt guilty that he was driving her to the emergency room again. He had done so much for her already.

She found herself studying his profile in the dim light of the dashboard. She was positive any of the women that had been in the tavern tonight would say he was gorgeous. Many of them had their eyes glued to him while he was dancing.

Collin took his eyes off the road to glance at her for a moment. The lights of an oncoming car flickered across his features. She could see that they were questioning. She knew he had caught her studying him.

"I want to thank you for everything," Madison said softly. "You've really been a blessing to me."

She pressed her head against the back of her seat thinking how his presence at the tavern tonight had once again been coincidental. He was there when she needed him again. The word, *rescue,* popped into her mind. She winced. *She was not a damsel in distress to be saved again and again. She had always been able to take care of herself! Until Nick died it seemed.*

"Madison?" He put his hand on her arm.

His touch felt good. For a moment she felt a lick of heat soar through her body as an image crept seductively into her brain; his arms were around her waist and she was looking up into his magnificent brown eyes while they were dancing. "I was just thinking about Eden," she whispered, keeping her eyes on the road. "I hope she'll be alright."

She shook her head to clear her unwanted thoughts. *It was called transference.* She had read about this on the internet. She shouldn't trust these romantic feelings she was having for Collin. Besides that it had only been a little over a year since Nick passed away. Yet Collin's face seemed to be popping into her head all the time now. And into her dreams. *Should I tell him? Should I let him know I dreamt about him several nights ago? He's my therapist after all. Nick has only been gone a year. Somehow it feels like I'm betraying Nick in some way.*

Collin cleared his throat. "The lifesaver's daughter must be out roaming the beach tonight looking for her lover." He glanced at her again as his mouth curved into a smile. "Someone told me he's seen the ghost several times when he was out walking along the beach near the lighthouse."

"How did he know it was a ghost?

"Apparently he was out one night with his wife strolling along the beach, when they saw a woman coming towards them carrying a lantern. They both said 'hello' to her as she passed. When they realized she'd only been wearing a long nightgown, they turned to look at her again and she was gone. Anyway that's the story he gave."

"Did he go back with his equipment?"

"Equipment?"

"I guess people who are into serious ghost hunting use equipment." She gave him a weak smile. "At least that's what I assume. I've watched *Ghost Hunter* a few times."

Collin nodded. "I would bet on it. I think his biggest problem is with his wife. He said she's threatened to turn him into a ghost if he doesn't spend more time with his family."

"Is this one of your patients?

"No, he's my mechanic, but I'd like to get him into therapy. I think he could use some counseling just to keep on the earth plane at times."

"The world we live in is an amazing place. There are so many mysteries out there."

"So you're one of those…"

"One of those?"

"One of those people who appreciate a good mystery. Why what did you think I was going to say?" he gently teased.

"I suppose I do love mysteries, especially…" She paused perhaps a little too long, thinking of Vincent and Oliver and the spirit bag that she'd found in her apartment.

"Are you going to tell me?"

"Of course," she said feeling anxiety ripple through her again. "Someday I will." *I have a feeling someday I will tell you everything, Collin Richardson*, she thought. *And I think you will be more than just a little surprised.*

"THE ROOM SPINS WHEN I MOVE MY HEAD. I also feel like throwing up. Isn't that how you felt, Madison?"

"I also had a headache," Madison offered, realizing the room Eden had been placed in at the hospital was the same one she had been given. "Try not to worry too much. From what I read it's not unusual for pregnant women to get dizzy. You have more blood in your body because of the baby. You were also dancing up a storm. Add to that the fact you eat like a bird."

"There's also a chance it could be anemia, or my blood pressure." Eden made a face.

Madison gave her a reassuring smile. "Don't worry they'll figure it out. You'll be going home in no time."

"What if the baby is not fine?" Eden's eyes were filled with worry. "I've already had one miscarriage."

"Why didn't you tell me?"

"I didn't want to upset you. You had so many other things on your mind at the time."

A nurse walked in just then and gave them both a cheery smile. "If you need anything, just let me know," she said, straightening the covers again.

"I could use an extra pillow." Eden sat up as the nurse tucked a pillow behind her head.

When the nurse left, Eden turned to Madison. "How did you get here so fast? You didn't have the keys to my car." Eden gave her a weak smile. "I assume it must have been Collin who drove you here."

Madison could feel her face grow warm. She was thankful that Anna appeared in the doorway moments later. Her landlady walked over to the bed and kissed Eden's forehead.

"Thank goodness you're alright!" Anna exclaimed.

"They're still running tests, mom."

"I just hope you won't be confined to your bed."

Eden winced. "What do you mean?"

"In the old days, when women were in danger of having a miscarriage, they were told not to get out of bed. Back then they didn't have the drugs to help stop premature labor. They waited and prayed. I know one woman who had triplets who spent six months on her back so that her babies could grow to term safely." Anna frowned. "Why don't we talk about this later? I'm sure everything will be just fine."

"I'm okay discussing it, Mom. I'm just trying to shrink the dragon here."

"Shrink the dragon? Don't tell me you're having hallucinations, too!"

"It's Danny's expression for knowing all the facts so you can face them... then they don't overwhelm you."

"So your husband is a dragon slayer, now? I really wish he'd get a regular job. He hasn't sold a screen play yet!"

"Shrink them not kill them, mom. According to some of my kindergarten fans, a percentage of evil dragons can be rehabilitated." Eden pulled the covers up to her chin and frowned. "I can't help but think about all the chemicals we put into the environment and how they can affect pregnant women. There's a study done on a town near the Dow Chemical plant that sits on the shore of the St. Clair River. It shows that a greater percentage of little girls were born in the area than boys. They think a chemical or combination of chemicals in the water near the plant is interfering with hormones and gestation. I wonder what the percentage's are?"

"Percentages?" Anna grabbed a tissue out of a box near the bed and wiped her glasses. "In this day and age people want a computer generated model of the problem in question and .appropriate graphics so they can treat themselves. In the old days they just had to listen to their doctor. They couldn't just Google up a page on their smart phone."

"Well in the old days, the doctor was god, or in your case, a goddess, mom."

"I just would have liked it if you would not have waited so long to have this baby so I would have more energy to enjoy it with!"

"Mom, you need to work out more. There's a water aerobics class at the high school you can join."

"Why would I want to do water aerobics after you've told me how many chemicals there are in the water system?"

"I'd love to see you start some kind of an exercise program."

Anna frowned, "I guess even a goddess needs a kick in the pants once in a while!"

"It's never too late," Eden said. She winced in pain, just as another nurse entered the room.

CHAPTER NINETEEN

Wanda sat up in bed and quickly turned on the light. Perspiration made her face feel damp and sticky. She rubbed her eyes then took a drink of water out of the plastic bottle that she'd left on her nightstand overnight. There had been a boy and girl in her dream. They had been sitting beside a river near a forest. *Were they in some kind of danger?*

She decided to get dressed and go for a walk on the beach. The fresh air always cleared her head and helped her to think. After putting her clothes on, she slipped out the front door of her condo. While walking across the parking lot, she noticed that the breakwater in front of the building was lined with fishermen. She glanced at the playground that faced the harbor. It was deserted except for one lone figure with a white beard sitting on a bench.

The Scotsman's presence on the beach had caught her by surprise one morning three years earlier. She had gone out to take her usual walk on a beautiful Sunday morning and saw Robert sitting on one of the swing sets that overlooked the harbor. His bright blue eyes had crinkled with good humor when she'd said 'good day' to him then stared at his beautiful snow white beard for a moment with a delighted smile on her face. Robert McDuff sitting on a child's swing set in the middle of the summer, with the sand dunes sweeping the shoreline behind him and the lake in front of him, made quite a picture in his tan shorts, with red suspenders and plaid beret. The jolly man on vacation would be an appropriate caption for any pictures taken of Mr. McDuff that day.

If she had any concerns about Robert's presence on the playground that sat on the harbor at the north end of town, her worries evaporated when she found out he'd been an inspector for Scotland Yard for over thirty years. Robert had specialized in child abductions. He'd moved to Michigan after his only daughter had married an American. Robert had followed the young couple to the states to be with his grandchildren when he retired after his wife had died.

Robert was now a very dear friend. Although she was older than him by almost a decade they certainly enjoyed each other's company. He had invited her to his home and had cooked dinner for her numerous times. Afterwards they'd sat on the deck overlooking the lake behind his cottage and had talked well into the evening while watching the sun go down together. She had told him about Poland, the country where she'd been born. She had been surprised and delighted to discover, that Robert's maternal grandfather had been Polish.

"And another interesting bit o information for ye is that America almost had a king," Robert had exclaimed that evening before giving her a grin and downing a shot of very strong whiskey. Finally raising one eyebrow, he added, "did you know, my dear lady, that general George Washington once asked Bonnie Prince Charles to be King of America when your founding fathers were seeking a dear lad for that job." Robert made a face and shook his head. "But alas, he declined. I think it was because the colonists were a wee bit too tame for him."

"Too tame?" She'd almost choked on her tea. Robert had to pat her back. It was just before they both broke into peals of laughter.

She greeted several fishermen standing along the breakwater as she continued her brisk walk. "Catch anything?" she asked.

"We've caught several big ones," the younger of the two men held up a tiny sunfish he'd just caught. He gave her a smile.

The older man with a moustache fishing beside him nodded his head at her in greeting. His eyes were a deep blue. They reminded her of Madison's.

Wanda frowned. Madison hadn't called her in several days. She assumed her niece was busy helping Eden with the nursery for her baby. Apparently after the scare last week, which sent Eden to the hospital, the doctors were certain there was no danger to the baby now. *Was it just a coincidence that both Madison and Eden had passed out?*

When she returned to the condo she made herself a cup of coffee and sat down with her laptop. After going on the internet, she checked her face book page, then headed to the shower. She was having dinner with Robert later at his cottage on one of the small lakes near Eagle Bay. But before that could happen she had a bit of work to do.

"AYE, HER NAME WAS MARIA CLEMENTINA SOBIESKA. The Princess was from one of the richest noble families in Europe. She was the granddaughter of John Sobieski III, the King of Poland. She was also the mother of our dearly beloved Bonnie Prince Charles Stuart," Robert said, picking up the wine bottle that sat on the table in front of them. "Would yer like another drink, Wanda?"

Wanda shook her head. "No thank you, Robert. But I must say the dinner was superb. You are a wonderful cook and a great host."

"I might add that the homemade pierogis were excellent, too, Wanda. They went very well with the lamb."

"Robert, thank you so much for inviting me over for dinner again. You know how much I love it here at your cottage. I feel much more relaxed tonight. This is much better than sitting home alone and wondering and worrying. "

"What are you worrying so hard about, my dear friend?"

"I've been having dreams, Robert. Some of them have been very terrible."

"My sister, Laurna, had dreams," Robert said, "Mum didn't know how to help her. She dreamt of our grandmother dying several weeks before she actually died and our granny had not even been sick."

"I've been having dreams for many years. Many times, I sense the people I dream about are in danger and I can't help them. Sometimes it makes me so worried that I can't sleep!"

Now, my dear friend, you must not make yourself responsible

for what you are seeing. You will surely make your self sick!"

"What can I do to stop these images that play in my head? Am I crazy, Robert?"

"You are far from crazy, my friend, in fact you are one of the sanest people I know with a mind that is filled with much clarity and compassion. Wanda, I do believe you have a gift." Robert was silent for a moment as he stared into his glass. Finally he raised his eyes to her. "We used several psychics to help in our detective work. They did indeed have a gift. They helped to bring much needed closure to families. But sometimes they suffered because of what they saw. Each new case seemed to take a part of them. Many could not continue to do the work at some point. My sister Laurna, was empathic. I don't want to alarm you with this Wanda, but I have something to show you."

Robert got up and went into one of the bedrooms. He came back with a manila envelope. For several moments he searched the contents while Wanda studied his face. What he was about to show her was causing him an enormous amount of pain.

"This is a letter that Laurna wrote. I found it among her things after she died." Robert handed the sheet of paper to her.

It looked like water stains had smeared the ink in several areas on the paper. *Were they Laurna's or Robert's tears?* The letter was a full page long, but a very emotional paragraph stood out to her, She wanted to weep for Robert's sister. She hoped Laurna was at peace now.

LIFE AS AN EMPATH WITHOUT SHIELDING IS EXTREME TORTURE BECAUSE YOU ARE NOT YOU ALL THE TIME...YOU BECOME THE PERSON YOU ARE TRYING TO HEAL ...IT'S AWFUL BECAUSE YOU FEEL THAT PERSON'S EMOTIONAL AND PSYCHOLOGICAL PAIN AND IT CAN BE SO OVERWHELMING THAT MOST OF THE TIME IT CAN BE PURE HELL. I HAVE NO CHOICE BUT TO ACCEPT THIS CROSS THAT I WAS BORN WITH. GOD PLEASE HELP ME!!! IS IT .MY DESTINY TO ABSORB PAIN AND SUFFERINGS FROM PEOPLE AROUND ME THE REST OF MY LIFE? FOR MANY YEARS .I NEVER KNEW I WAS AN EMPATH....SO I HAD BEEN DOING THIS ABSORPTION AUTOMATICALLY WITHOUT EVEN UNDERSTANDING

WHY I WAS FEELING SO BAD ...I'VE HAD A NUMBER OF MAJOR CLINICAL DEPRESSIONS IN TEN YEARS!! THOSE NEGATIVE EMOTIONS WERE NOT EVEN MINE!!! I AM A SPONGE!! I ABSORB EVERYTHING FROM MY ENVIRONMENT ...AND THE LAST TEN YEARS I HAVE BEEN LIVING IN THE LAND OF PSYCHIC HELL.

CHAPTER TWENTY

Madison took the slip of paper out of her purse. She read the first three lines of the poem again. *What could they possibly mean?* It felt like the poem was slowly unveiling itself to her and if she waited patiently she would finally understand its meaning; *I see you crying I wonder how my touch can soothe your heart. White shows so much against dark.* Yet several times in the past few days, after she'd read it over, she'd been filled with an incredible amount of despair she couldn't explain. *And the tears that came afterwards! Was she losing her mind?* Madison refolded the paper and put it back in her wallet, then glanced at her cell phone. She had an appointment with Collin at three and just enough time to take a quick shower. After paying her bill at the small deli, she walked down the street to her car.

It was a cloudy, windy day. Along the breakwater, she guessed close to a dozen fishermen were strung out in a line on the harbor wall trying their luck. She came to a stop in front of the Victorian, grabbed her things out of the car and made her way to the door of the upstairs apartment. On the way up the walk, the wind lashed at her, bringing with it drops of rain that pelted her face. When she made it inside, she headed to the bathroom, undressed, and ran the shower. The hot water felt good on her body. For several minutes the warmth of the water melted away all her thoughts and she stood luxuriating in it, allowing it to soak into her and to work on her aching muscles.

She heard the phone ring in the bedroom. She was certain whoever it was would leave a message if it was important, but the conditioned response of answering a ringing phone had not left her. She grabbed a towel and went to the nightstand where the house phone sat.

She was disappointed to discover that Collin had called to cancel her appointment in therapy that afternoon. Apparently his son had been in an accident playing baseball and had been rushed to the hospital. Collin was driving home to be with him.

"Devin is asking for me." Collin's voice sounded tense and worried. "I have to reschedule your appointment. I may have to stay here with him. I might not be back in town for awhile."

An overwhelming feeling of disappointment poured over her. What if Collin decided to leave his practice because of his son and move back to Grosse Ponte? What would she do then? Dr. Bishop had stayed away much longer than they all anticipated. Because of that she'd grown to trust Collin. She thought of the delighted look on his face when she'd given him the collar she'd found for Goliath at one of the gift shops down the street from the gallery. That day they'd stayed in his office talking almost forty five minutes longer than her normal session because she'd been his last patient. Those few minutes with Collin had somehow lifted her out of her depression as they talked about a multitude of every day things, movies they both liked and other things that normal people talked about that did not involve death or grieving or the holocaust for that matter.

She slowly got dressed and headed to the kitchen. She turned on the television and sat down at the kitchen table. Once again a deep feeling of despair began to wrap itself around her and held her captive. The weatherman was reporting severe weather heading for Eagle Bay. She glanced out the window. The sky was much dimmer to the east. A storm was definitely brewing.

ANNA BURGESS WAS STANDING on her porch when Madison finally went outside to get her mail. Anna was wearing a rain coat and cradling her normally snow white cat, Sophia, who was spackled with mud. Sophia was purring happily in her arms. Anna sighed and hugged the cat closer. 'I'm surprised she's not struggling to jump out of my arms and go to that tom cat whose been coming round to visit her every night.'

"She looks pretty happy. I hate to say it, but I think she's already had a date with him, Anna, if I'm guessing correctly." Madison gave Anna a tired smile. She was thankful her nausea had subsided.

"Sophia, what am I going to do with you?" Anna caressed the cat and then pushed her inside the door of the house. I'll have to clean her up later and she won't like that very much." Anna turned back to her. "By the way, the weather channel is reporting eighty mile an hour winds on Lake Michigan today. Everyone is down at the beach watching the waves. Apparently the breakers are hitting the revetment and are taller than the lighthouse. The boys have their surfing gear out. I think I'm going down there to watch. Want to come?"

"I was just walking out for the mail. I'll have to get my wallet. Maybe it would do me some good to get out for awhile. I'll be just a few minutes, Anna." Madison turned and headed back to the house.

A half hour later, with Madison in tow, Anna stopped her car in the parking area near the beach. A group of die-hard surfers were out on the lake just past the break walls. They were dressed in black neoprene suits, a far cry from the stereo-type of surfers in bright colored swim trunks who plied the waves in Hawaii or California. But they were enjoying themselves, none-the-less. Madison knew this particular group were part of a surfing club. They had been going out on the Great Lake for quite some time.

"I don't think the freighter captains are enjoying the weather as much as these guys," Anna exclaimed, as a huge wave shot up near the lighthouse at the point of the breakwater.

"Neither do I." Madison replied, growing anxious as she watched the foaming water burst into fountains against the breakwater only to recede and hit it again and again. She always loved watching the waves, but today they were upsetting her and she was feeling more and more terrified, for some reason, filled with a fear she couldn't explain.

"Can you imagine what ships had to contend with in the past? They had no harbor of refuge like we have today, Anna."

"My goodness, can you imagine the sea sickness those people

experienced at times."

"Did I tell you about the interesting information that I came across on the shipwreck that I found in the water. The article was on the wall at the nautical museum in town. Apparently the schooner foundered in a storm. A woman died mysteriously on board the ship."

"How awful, Madison. Come to think of it, there should be more information at the museum if you know where to look," Anna gazed into the review mirror and smoothed her hair while she spoke. "If the ship wreck falls within a certain time frame you may be able to find out more about the woman. There were quite a number of journals at the museum that were kept by the Catholic priest who lived in the town during the logging era. From what I've read, Father Chabert was a saint to many people, especially the Indians. I've processed several of his journals for the historical society. Several years ago, we had a speaker at the museum talking about the lumbering era. She actually mentioned the priest."

MADISON PUT THE JOURNAL DOWN on the desk in the office of the museum and rubbed her eyes. She had been reading and taking notes for close to two hours in the dim light after Anna had gotten her a key to the museum. She put the diaries away, and headed up the steps of the old church. The main floor of the museum was dark and had the musty smell of old antiques. When she passed through the interior of the museum, she had the sensation she was in a time machine. The walls were covered in nautical artifacts from the 1800's. A life boat sat in the middle of the main floor filled with gear that had been used for rescues. Life saving vests and ship's anchors were placed around it, along with a Lyle gun that resembled a small canon. She'd read that the device was used to send lines to foundering vessel so that breeches buoys could be hooked up to them like swings to rescue the people on board during storms.

Her head began to pound ferociously as she drew near the life boat. Within seconds the room went into a wicked spin. She let out a groan, feeling a tide of fear, then nausea rise in her stomach. She felt like throwing up. For several frightened moments, she stood bracing herself against the side of the boat and felt like vomiting again as pains ripped through her abdomen. When the wave of dizziness subsided, she made her way to a bench that was placed against the wall and sat down. Closing her eyes she leaned back against the bench. Another moan escaped her throat when she opened them and the room took off in a crazy whirl. *How could she possibly drive home like this?*

ANNA HANDED MADISON A CUP OF chamomile tea and sat down at the kitchen table in the upstairs apartment. "I have some medication downstairs that I think will help, but it might make you very sleepy. Some of my patients told me they felt like zombies after taking it. I'll get it for you when I go down." Anna took a sip of her own tea and set it down. "You do look like you're feeling better. You don't look as ashen as you looked when I picked you up at the museum, thank goodness. I'll drive you down there in the morning so you can get your car. Are you sure you don't want to go to emergency?

"I feel much better now that I'm home."

Anna shrugged. "By the way, what's with this zombie apocalypse thing, lately? Good grief, don't we have enough on the evening news to scare us?"

"Halloween is coming in the next couple of weeks. We'll see lots of strange creatures out on the streets soon. Have you ever been to Romeo? There's a street there that is decorated to the hilt every Halloween. If I was a small child and lived on that street, I would definitely have a problem getting to sleep.".

"Have you had any problems sleeping lately?"

"I've been waking up at three a.m. like clockwork. I can't sleep so I write."

"I thought you were painting? What are you working on? Eden will be happy to hear someone's writing. She's been dealing with writer's block, lately. Of course all of her focus has been on the baby."

"I told you about the shipwreck we found. I've been researching it. I was hoping the priest you told me had mentioned it in his journals."

"The priest kept wonderful diaries of what was happening in the village, didn't he?" Anna sat down at the table and dipped her tea bag into her cup. "I remember reading something about him raising a young native boy whose mother tried to kill herself."

"It was horrible how the priest died. I read his obituary in an old newspaper."

"Fires were terrible back then. All the buildings were made of lumber. Thousands of gorgeous old hotels in Michigan have been lost to fires. Just think of the Grand Hotel on Mackinac Island and how wonderful it is. There were hundreds of hotels that were similar to it, but on a smaller scale. Jonathon's grandmother actually built several of those beautiful buildings. At the time it was unusual for a woman to own anything, let alone be responsible for building it. After his grandfather died Lydia took over his lumbering business. She was truly a remarkable woman."

"There are so many remarkable people that we don't normally hear about. Father Chabert reminds me of a priest in Poland named Father Kolbe. This man gave his life for another prisoner in Auschwitz who had children so he would not be executed. I learned about him on my tour there several years ago as well as a man called Witold Pilecki. There was also a very heroic woman named Irena Sendler who saved two thousand Jewish children."

Anna shook her head sadly. "Those pedophile priests have cast a horrible shadow on the truly saintly men who really live their faith. Even though I'm Episcopalian, I have the deepest respect for some of the Catholic priests of old and the innocent men who have to deal with the scandal now. People don't realize how many clergy were murdered by the Gestapo in Poland because they posed a threat to their power. In Germany many Catholic priests who stood against the Nazi's were threatened with death, and interred in concentration camps. I can't imagine what the Soviets did to priests after they took over Poland.

Anna finally stood up and walked over to the kitchen sink, depositing her teacup in it. "I have to get up early tomorrow morning, dear, so I need to hit the sack right away. If you feel dizzy or sick in any way at all again, call me. Okay?"

For several minutes Madison sat at the kitchen table after Anna left. She could hear trees branches rattling outside the window as the wind grew stronger. For some reason she was feeling unbearably sad. She headed to her bedroom. She laid down on her bed for a moment and closed her eyes. The cadence of the wind outside the Victorian was strangely soothing as tears began to stream down her face as she fell asleep.

In the dream she was standing in the middle of a clearing waiting for someone. All around her pine trees loomed against the darkening sky like sentinels. Anxiety rippled through her body as she searched for familiar stars that would help her find her way home again. But back to where? Where was home? Madison groaned in her sleep as questions filled her head. Were they watching her? Had they seen her leave the house? Did they follow her? She heard an owl hoot in the trees near the forest. Her heart skipped a beat. Then she spotted a figure standing by the stream in the moonlight. Without thinking she ran to it. She put her arms around the man's waist pressing her face against his back and took in the acrid scent of smoke and grease. She crinkled her nose. Why didn't he turn to face her? Why was he just standing there looking down at the reflection of the moon in the stream as though in a trance? And why oh why didn't he gather her in his arms and lift her high into the air like he always did? What was wrong? When he finally turned to her, and she caught a glimpse of his face in the moonlight, she let out a gasp. Even in the shadows she could make out the purple bruises and the torn swollen lip. She knew in her heart it was all because of her!

She came awake. A small scream escaped her lips. When she finally opened her eyes she was trembling. She reached for the notebook lying on the nightstand beside her bed and began to record the dream. Closing the book again, she put it down and noticed that the medicine Anna had given her was not where she remembered putting it next to the lamp. She must have knocked the vial onto the floor. She searched the carpet beside the bed. Nothing! Sliding onto the floor, she peered under the dust ruffle pulling out several socks and a small plastic storage box for shoes. Her heart skipped a beat. Once again tears began to fill her eyes-- only this time it wasn't because of the dream. It was because of the photo album that was wedged between the mattress and the wall. She'd slept with the white book trimmed with gold leaf in her arms the night of Nick's funeral. Had it been there all this time?

She was kneeling besides the bed looking at the photos when the room began to spin and she grew violently ill again.

CHAPTER TWENTY ONE

Anna Burgess called Wanda at ten o'clock the following morning. "I found Madison unconscious in her bedroom. The ambulance is here right now!" Anna exclaimed, trying to catch her breath.

Wanda gasped. "What happened?"

"I gave her some medicine for her nausea last night. I called her this morning when I got up. She didn't answer the phone, so I used my key to get into her apartment. I found her lying unconscious beside her bed and called EMS."

"Thank you for everything, Anna. I'll get down to the hospital as soon as I can!" After calling Robert, Wanda looked up the number of Madison's therapist.

"Mr. Richardson is not available at the present time, but you can leave a message for him. It's not clear when he'll be back just yet," a woman from his answering service explained."

"Please let him know I called. Madison Andrews is one of his patients and she's in Community Hospital again."

"I'll get hold of him as soon as I can," the woman said before hanging up.

Wanda made her way into the small kitchen. She poured herself a glass of wine and took a sip. Just then she heard a knock at the door. She peered out the window. Robert was standing on her porch with a worried look on his face,

"I've knocked several times! Had you not heard me?" he said

when she finally let him in.

"No I didn't Robert! How did you get here so fast? Do you want me to drive?

"Nay, I will drive. I don't think you can concentrate very well right now, my dear woman. I think I must take charge for the moment."

Dear God! Not again! Wanda felt shaky and weak as she peered down at Madison lying in the hospital bed. She pushed Madison's hair gently away from her face, and studied her niece's features. It looked like Madison was only sleeping, then she noticed the grimaces. *Was she in pain?*

Wanda sat in the room with Madison for two hours, before deciding to go to the chapel to pray. When she returned a half hour later she found one of Madison's doctors standing beside the bed with a nurse.

"We'll let you know if we come up with something. Right now it looks like all her tests have come back normal, which is very odd considering the bruising on her arms and legs, Mrs. Kowalski."

"Bruising?"

"Yes, we're still trying to determine what caused it."

Wanda shook her head. "I don't understand, doctor."

"Actually we don't understand either," Dr. Martin said, putting a pen in his pocket. "The bruises were apparently not there when she was brought in this morning. We found them around her wrists and some near her ankles."

"Bruises? This is all sounding very strange, doctor."

"It is indeed. We will definitely be consulting some specialists. We plan on keeping her in the hospital until we can clear this up."

After the doctor left, Wanda placed a kiss on Madison's forehead, and slipped out of the room. She walked down the hall to the patient lounge where Robert was waiting for her.

"I need to locate Madison's insurance card for the hospital," she told him. "I'd like to come back later, Robert. Right now I need some time to think."

Robert nodded. 'We can stop by her apartment."

WHEN THEY GOT TO THE VICTORIAN, Wanda knocked on Anna's front door.

"Just let me know what else you need," Anna said, handing her a key to the upstairs apartment. "I'll take it to the hospital myself. How is she now? Are there any changes?"

"No… she's the same."

"This is all so unfortunate." Anna winced. "I gave her some medication for her dizziness last night. A coma can be drug induced, but there's no reason to believe she took any drugs other than what I gave her. And I doubt this drug would cause something like this. The dizziness sounds like an important factor, yet I feel it's benign. Madison told me they tested her at the hospital several weeks ago and found no abnormalities in her brain. She was lying beside her bed unconscious when I walked in. There was a notebook and photo album open. She must have been looking at them when she passed out. I left them lying where they were.

"THE DESCRIPTIONS ARE WONDERFUL in the story she is writing, Robert," Wanda said flipping through the notebook she had taken from Madison's apartment. She read a paragraph out loud to Robert.

"Wanda, does it not occur that your niece is foundering like this woman she is writing about?"

"Madison has always been a very sensitive person, Robert. She dealt with some depression after Joseph died. I think she had it because she came to the full realization of what happened to her grandfather during the war. It was all so ugly and evil. No one who is human can look at what happened and not be affected by it."

"Aye, Wanda. You told me she loved her grandfather very much and knowing of the indignities he suffered she could only feel the pain herself."

"Robert there is much I need to tell you about Joseph and Madison and about what happened when she was a child. But there is something else that worries me. Do you think she was actually attacked? You must read the story she's written."

"Wanda I believe we have to sit down and sort this all out. I've an important meeting with someone who may be able to help your niece. I must go now to meet with her. I hope you don't mind.

I'll call you when I get back." Robert got up from the couch and grabbed his jacket.

"What would I do without you, Robert? Thank you so much for everything you've done for me."

Robert looked down at Wanda for several moments. Finally he put his hand on her cheek. "It is my pleasure, my dear friend. Now let's find out what is plaguing your niece!

Wanda watched him open the front door and leave. Afterwards she found the notebook she had collected from Madison's apartment.

****

THE SHIPWRECK

Suddenly the idea that this man was trying to assault her when the ship was foundering was so absurd Ananda felt like laughing hysterically. In deep anguish she began to recite a short prayer she had composed while she was in boarding school at St. Mary's; her voice growing louder and louder.

"The lord is my navigator! Though, I sail in the face of the tempest I know I am secure for I shall forever be guided in to the safe harbor of his arms. The Lord is my lifesaver. He will trudge the sands to find me and will not rest until I am found. The Lord shall forever be my anchor, my hope and the brilliant light I seek upon every shore."

She cried out in pain when he caught her hair as she tore away from him when he tried to kiss her. Her eyes flooded with tears when her head began to throb with pain. Seeing her chance, she lunged for the doorway, and tripped, hitting her face on the floor. When she tried to stand up again she was once again thrown onto the deck when the boat started to reel from side to side. She closed her eyes, feeling the fire in her bruised and swelling cheek. Tears began to stream down her face when she looked up to see him coming at her. Suddenly without any warning he was thrown backwards with such force she thought at first one of God's warrior angels had come down from heaven to help her. But the ship had shifted its position. It sent him slamming into the wall of the cabin and she herself was tossed into the wall of the cabin.

She felt a sharp pain spread across her back and legs. Ribbons of darkness seemed to dance and sway around her in a growing fog. For several moments she lay on the floor of the cabin with the wind knocked out of her. She could not speak when the crewmen approached her. She went completely limp when one of the men touched her wrist. Gathering her into his arms, he hoisted her off the floor and very gently set her down on the lumpy mattress that had been her bed.

"She's very sick, Tobin. The old sailor shook his head, weariness and fear knotting the muscles on his weather-beaten face. "I just pray she'll survive the lines," he added in a whisper.

Ananda was slipping further into darkness. Was she dying?

The crewmen fought hard to keep their balance against the roll of the schooner. One of them began to pray out loud. As if to answer any questions they had about their chances of surviving the storm, the boat gave a tremendous heave, sending them all tumbling to the wooden floor.

Once again, Ananda fought an army of shadows as she sprawled across the floor of the boat. Perhaps it would be better to die than face the remainder of her life alone. She was certain she would never be allowed to live peacefully in the small harbor town. If her family did not accept him they would make a life elsewhere!

Her conviction gave her strength. "I think I can walk, she whispered to one of the sailors.

The crewmen carefully lifted her under each arm and helped her make her way through the cabin. When they emerged on the rocking deck, they fastened a rope around her waist then around her wrists and ankles lashing their bodies together so she would not be washed overboard. Even with the added safety of the rope every step she took was a perilous one. She struggled to keep her footing on the heaving boat while the wind tore savagely at her tattered bedclothes. It screamed obscenely in her ears and sent nuggets of hail, like buckshot, biting into her face and neck. Only the crew man's firm grasp kept her from being thrust headlong into the boiling lake when the schooner pitched and rolled from side to side.

Ananda shuddered with fear as icy blasts of air penetrated her *body, chilling her to the bone as she struggled to keep her footing on the slippery deck. She realized the northwest wind had kicked up yet another storm that ripped across the lake with incredible fury attempting to tumble everything in its path. She had heard many a story about Nor'easters blowing up so suddenly on the lake they left no escape. She knew she had taken a dangerous chance making her trip home so late in the year. Yet she had been more that willing to take the risk. She now realized the terrible danger she had put herself in by choosing to leave Chicago so abruptly. The small schooner was no match for the driving wind and water. Pummeled mercilessly by the cresting waves the ship had been driven onto a sandbar and now stood aground unable to make the safety of the shoreline. It was now lethally exposed to the vicious storm that threatened to tear it apart.*

She could make out lights in the distance, and through the darkness and roar of the surf, muffled shouts could be heard on the shore. It could only mean one thing they were close to a town and the possibility of rescue.

She watched the crew work feverishly to bring down what was left of the shredded sails that still caught the wind and sent the ship tilting at dangerous angles. Water thwarted them at every turn. Great tentacles of water enlivened by the wind reached into every crevice of the ship.

Once again the realization that he had paid no heed to the treacherous storm tore brutally through her senses. The realization that he too would be on deck seeking the safety of the rigging was almost too much for her. She was almost certain he had not been part of the crew. Suddenly she was overwhelmed with a sense of betrayal. She hoped with all her heart she was wrong. And yet, moments later when she once again glanced beyond the small group of men who had gathered around her, she spied him at the far end of the boat. Completely drenched, he was almost unrecognizable. Had he been planning this assault for some time? She shivered with revulsion when she realized he was moving closer. She began to tremble, and when he was within a few feet, her knees began to buckle. It seemed she could only watch helplessly as he reached for her arm, just as the rudderless ship swung to the left sending them slamming into the side of the deckhouse. The last thing she heard was what sounded like a muffled shot before a wave came crashing down on top of them. She gasped wildly for air and felt her body being dragged across the icy deck. Cloudy images, like glints of light on cracking ice, skated across her foundering mind.

Lines were snapping dangerously close to her head as more and more of the shredded sails above were stripped from the masts exposing the skeleton-like remains of the rigging. The schooner once proud, now badly wounded, could only seem to groan eerily while its canvas was being devoured by the savaging wind.

Ananda tried desperately to make out the faces that were part of the whirling shadows. Intuitively, she recognized the touch of the crewmen who had carried her onto the deck. With frozen hands they pulled her limp body into the rigging overhead. Water poured over the glistening planks as the men worked furiously to secure her to one of the swaying masts. Suddenly a line snapped beside them: the jagged piece of iron it still carried grazed her temple just missing one of her eyes. The open wound stung in the icy wind. Her mother's voice seemed to echo around her just as the ship listed to one side, sending her swinging crazily through the turbulent air and then plunging low over the snarling teeth of the lake.

"You're always looking for stars, Ananda."

Ananda managed a choking laugh thinking of her mother's well-used words to her. There were no stars in this godforsaken world, nothing to warm her freezing tattered soul! The sky above her was filled with a battalion of brutal looking clouds, blotting out any ray of light or hope. It seemed they raced across the heavens to some distant battle beyond the horizons, taking the moon and stars captive along the way.

She was cold, so cold. The wind raked over her body like the surging tides. She started to pray feverishly, her rose-hued lips turning blue in the numbing air. It seemed terror, like the freezing lines, held her body suspended against the sky as though she were a sacrifice to an angry god. In the bleakness of her despair, she pictured herself frozen to the wooden mast; her rigid body smooth and white as marble, her lusterless eyes and ashen lips hardened by the frosty wind; while her pale hair fanned out about her like a lake fern. Would children find her body on the beach one day and think her a mermaid when she washed up some warm summer

135

afternoon?

She'd seen a young boy who had drowned in the half-frozen waters of Lake Michigan being brought back into town tied to the back of a pony cart one day when she had been a child. She had stood watching with the crowd of curious townspeople as his naked and bloated body had been wheeled past. He had been taken to his mother's cottage where minutes later heart wrenching sobs had shattered the icy calm of a November morning. She would never forget the dead boy's face. The terrifying seconds of his drowning had seemed printed for all eternity on the doughy adolescent features that stared sightlessly at the sky. The silence of the townspeople who had stood with bowed heads on the beach had seemed somehow obscene in contrast to the boy's wide-eyed terror. Shivers tore down her spine. She remembered the horrifying vision from her childhood all too well. She had been sick of mind and heart for days afterwards, unable to concentrate on anything as the Northwest wind screamed through the small town and haunted her sleep with images of death.

Every now and then, below the threshold of the roaring wind Ananda thought she heard the tinkle of voices. She was certain she had heard a baby cry. Images of a newborn child flashed through her mind while a portion of the wooden mast above her, splintered sending pieces of well-baptized wood and searing pain ripping into her shoulder. The wind snatched her cries of anguish, carrying them off like a marauding vulture before they were allowed to mature. Barely able to focus because of the pain, Ananda picked out the glow of a bonfire on the distant shore while blood oozed from her wounded shoulder. Her breathing became even more labored when she spied the twinkle of lanterns nearby. The cold blustering air seemed to tear at her lungs with each breath she took.

On the glistening deck below her she watched in horror, as one of the main stays snapped. The ice covered line was razor sharp and lethal as it cracked like a bullwhip, threatening to slice anything in its path before writhing serpent-like across the planking in a demonic dance of uncontrolled fury. Another pain ripped through her shoulder making her cry out again. Searching for comfort, she could only gnash her teeth helplessly when she spied the crewman who had rescued her dangling in the rigging nearby. Their faces were bloodless in the anemic light. They hung from the icy lines like corpses, while the squall hammered them into the wood of the foremast.

Tears flooded her eyes as she searched the churning shadows for her attacker. Just the thought of him was every bit as painful as the freezing rope that cut into her wrists and seemed to slice the flesh from her ankles. A hatred like nothing she had experienced before consumed her. Were all men thieves? If not out to steal a woman's heart, then out to steal her spirit? Gasping wildly for air, Ananda started to choke when she was forced to swallow a mouthful of bitter spray while watching the icy crucifixions before her.

She thought of her baby again and relived a moment she had spent in almost worst agony, perched on a wave of excruciating pain, looking down into a dark deathly chasm, then watching in horror as a part of her life had been carried away forever, in bloody rags, as the storm of labor had ended. Slowly slipping out of consciousness, she once again dreamt of the boy she loved and pictured herself being gathered into the safety of his waiting arms while the storm claimed more and more of the sinking ship.

Suddenly from somewhere in the shadows near her she heard a voice strain against the deafening roar of the lake, its sound bringing her back to reality. She tried to raise her head, caught a glimpse of movement within the rigging and knew there was a boat out to save them and crewmen who were getting poised to greet the rescuers. Then she heard the shot. It could only mean one thing; a breeches buoy was being prepared to carry them off the ship. But even as the possibility of rescue seemed imminent she found herself drifting farther and farther away caught in a numbing haze of sorrow and shock. Yes, Lord, let the lake take me, she thought, feeling the numbness in her face and fingers spreading throughout her body and soul. Let the lake take me and place me where you will for my life has been as turbulent as the waves and my heart longs for a peaceful harbor where gentle waters shall bathe me and carry me beyond the darkest of clouds.

Suddenly she felt icy hands move along her bruised and battered face. In that instant, the memory of her assault gripped her and she tensed every muscle in her freezing body, feeling spasms ripple through her stiffened limbs. Again she felt hands upon her and the flutter of fingers upon her swollen mouth. She tried to raise her head, feeling its tired weight tilting her forward, and pictured herself hurtling to the deck below. She felt an emptiness consume her, leaving no words or images to be retrieved from the recesses of her memories, except that of John's face. For a brief moment, she felt him beside her, sharing her pain as she hung upon the icy mast.

As the schooner broke apart beneath her, it gave one deafening protest that thundered in the wind. Ananda heard screams echo across the turbulent lake. Together with the ravaged ship they were brutally scattered in the stormy, godless night.

CHAPTER TWENTY TWO

The traffic was heavy on I-75 as Collin drove north. The sky overhead was a dismal grey that was broken up periodically by lines of con trails that reminded him of a shattered mirror. There was no denying the pain he was feeling at the moment. Madison was in the hospital again. She was the only reason he was going back to Eagle Bay. If not for her, he would be packing up his belongings and driving home to stay near his son.

An old song by the group "America" called *Horse with No Name* played on the stereo while he drove. It was ironic, because at the moment, he felt like he was *in* the desert and sand was filling him up and lulling him into a kind of no-man's land. And that was just where he believed Madison was at that moment, in *no man's land*. The heaviness in his heart was almost unbearable. In the past few weeks Madison seemed to be making so much progress. And now this!

After a few hours of driving the interstate back to Eagle Bay, he was not surprised when his knee began to ache. Pulling over to a rest stop along the highway, south of Grayling, he got out of the car to stretch. After looking up at a sky, a sky that was growing darker and darker by the moment, he checked his cell phone. No one had called in the past several hours which he took as a good sign. Taking a deep breath, he finally shook his head to clear it.

Madison's case perplexed him like no other. He knew she had

been suffering from depression. In fact he had several patients who could not get out of bed in the morning and slept all day until they went on anti-depressants. He also knew that certain mental disorders including depression and catatonia could cause a state of unconsciousness similar to a coma. But something kept niggling at him. Madison's friend Eden came to mind quite often. The fact that Eden had collapsed on the dance floor two weeks ago was certainly pause for thought. Were the two cases connected?

While he was in Grosse Pointe for the last couple of days, he had also done more research on children of survivors. Madison was displaying all the symptoms of a child of a survivor who had generational post traumatic stress even though she wasn't Jewish. He knew she had internalized her grandfather's experiences. It had been heart breaking to read how not only the Jewish, but the Christian population of Poland had suffered during World War II because of the Nazi's. The country had faced more takeovers throughout its history than any other in Europe. She had told him in therapy that her grandfather, who had once been a prisoner in one of the concentration camps, had also been beaten and tortured by the communist government that came to power in Poland afterwards. The Soviet Union had been ruthless in its search for patriotic citizens who had been active in the Polish underground against the Germans as Madison's grandfather had been. It was a little known fact for decades that the Soviets pretending to be the country's liberators during WWII had tricked the Poles and secretly executed close to twenty thousand of their reserve officers in the Katyn Forest.

COLLIN MADE IT BACK TO EAGLE BAY in less than four hours. After pulling into town, he drove directly to Community General Hospital. When he walked into Madison's room, a shiver tore through him at the shock of seeing several IV's inserted into her arms.

Wanda's eyes looked red and swollen when she stood up to embrace him. He could feel the tears rising in his own eyes as she stood up to embrace him.

"How did this happen, Wanda?" He glanced at the bed and the dark shadows on the very thin and drawn face that lay against the white sheets. Madison was a shadow of the woman he had seen only a week ago. The change in her appearance was shocking!

"We don't know what is causing it. The doctors are doing every test they can to determine what steps to take. They haven't found anything so far. There's no sign she had a stroke and no trace of drugs in her blood. Anna said that when she found Madison she was lying beside her bed on the carpet. There was a photo album and her notebook lying open on top of her bedspread."

"What was she looking at in the photo album? Do you know?"

"I believe she was looking at a picture of herself standing between Nicholas and Joseph on her wedding day at church."

He walked over to the bed and put his hand on her arm. It felt very cold to his touch. He could see that Madison's face was set in a grimace.

"She wrote a story I think you should read," Wanda whispered. "I believe Madison may have been attacked at some point. The story starts out with an attempted rape."

"Raped?" *She never said anything to me in her sessions!* Suddenly he remembered the paintings that had been mutilated. *Had she been brutalized by the same person who destroyed the paintings?*

"I'll drop her notebook off at your office tomorrow so you can read it. When she comes out of this, she will need to talk. And she will come out of this! I know all of this looks bad, very bad," Wanda said looking him in the eyes. But I have to believe it's all for a reason."

COLLIN SHUT HIS LAPTOP AND TURNED the Weather Channel on. The weatherman was reporting an enormous storm heading for the East coast.

Goliath was lying on the carpet beside the sofa when he finally got up to go the kitchen. The dog wagged its tail when he stopped to pet his head and took a moment to straighten his new collar, a multi colored design with peace signs on it. Madison had given it to him just the week before.

Making his way into the kitchen he grabbed a soda out of the refrigerator and noticed that Madison's notebook was still sitting on the kitchen table where he'd left it. What he had read so far included a story about an attack on a woman. He wondered if Madison's aunt was right. Was Madison hiding the fact she'd been raped? Was her coma-like state a manifestation of the trauma she'd endured?

He decided to go back on the internet then thought better of it. He knew Goliath needed a walk. He also needed to clear his head. He grabbed Goliath's leash, a few paper towels and a plastic bag and took two aspirin. The weather had changed and he needed a warmer coat for his walk tonight.

EAGLE BAY WAS FILLED with the presence of an impending storm. The wind hit Collin full force as he walked out of the front door of the small house he'd rented on Kristin St. In the distance he could hear waves splashing on the pier. The moon was slightly visible in the night sky, shrouded by clouds that were scattered across the atmosphere like webs of gauze in preparation for Halloween. The trees were stark in the faint light. They spread their limbs across the sidewalk forming an archway of autumn wood that reminded him of the area near his childhood home in Detroit. Introspective and filled with a deep sense of unease he and Goliath made their way to the small city park that sat on the bay across the road.

After taking care of the dog he sat down on a park bench that overlooked the bay. He realized the wind had died down. It was just comfortable enough now to keep from him from getting sleepy.

What was happening at the moment seemed surreal. It felt as though the future was hanging over him like a moonless night that could be suffocating with its dark inky sky and lack of clarity. He knew he cared for Madison, perhaps a little too much for his own good. She was his patient and he had let her get under his skin to the point where he wasn't getting any sleep worrying about her. Yet he had to maintain his distance if he was to help her at all, that is if she came out of the coma. He could lose her at any time.

A man approached out of the darkness. The figure was smoking something and he could see a spark of orange light hanging in the air as it moved towards him. Goliath whined and stood up, pulling on the leash. Collin waited expectantly to see who else had taken a walk on such a blustery night.

"Good evening to yer," the voice said.

The man that appeared was the same man who had been at the hospital with Madison's aunt. Collin remembered his name was Robert.

"What a wonderful dog you have here, sir! May I? He looks like a cuddly teddy bear!" Robert's hand hovered over Goliath's head.

"Be my guest, he's very friendly."

Robert leaned forward stroking Goliath's huge head while gritting the cigar between his teeth. "Please don't tell Wanda you saw me smoking. I promised her I would quit." He gave Collin an enormous smile showing a row of yellow teeth.

Collin noticed that he had trimmed his beard. "I have several patients who are trying to quit. It's difficult, but not impossible. Have you tried the gum?"

"I've tried it all. Seems to me I like smoking too much. Perhaps I was a chimney in another life." Robert cocked his head to the side. "So yer one of her doctors," he exclaimed. It was more of a statement than a question. "Well, I have something to digest, so to speak. I think what's troubling Wanda's niece is not all in her mind."

"What do you mean?"

"What I mean is Madison is a very sensitive woman."

"Robert, has her condition changed much today? I'm afraid I can't discuss much more than that."

"You need not discuss it with me sir, but I'm telling you what I know. Madison's problems may not be what you think. It's not all in her head."

"Oh I agree there has to be an underlying medical reason. I'm not a psychiatrist Robert, but I have conferred with my colleagues who are psychiatrists."

"No my dear man, that's not what I mean." Robert sat down on the bench beside him. "I mean what is troubling Madison may not be because of her past, but rather because of someone in the past."

"You mean her grandfather?"

"No, I don't mean her grandfather. It's true, poor Joseph did indeed suffer as Wanda told me. His life was terrible from what I understand. I'm sure it affected his granddaughter who loved him dearly. The poor man went through so much only to have people make fun. Why if I had my way, I would *knock some blocks off*, a good old American term I've found very descriptive of how I feel after hearing what Joseph went through after coming to this country after the war. *"Dumb Polack jokes* indeed, I've heard enough of them, and the reason I kept my job, is because I am good natured and good at keeping my irritation to myself.

Robert took another puff off of his cigar and threw it on the sidewalk, then smashed it with his shoe. He picked it up and strode over to the garbage can, tossing it in with a flick of his wrist. He walked back to Collin and sat down.

My own grandfather was a Pole, mind you, I do know the history. I know that girl's grandfather went through unthinkable things that would kill an ordinary man, but Joseph was not an ordinary man. He was a saint for forgiving it all and doing what he did. I believe Madison loved her grandfather deeply. She shared his heartache, keeping it deep inside of her. She may not have witnessed the holocaust first hand, but she did indeed feel it and it impacted her life greatly, but not her spirit, sir." Robert's face was shrouded in shadows as he spoke. "I also believe that lass's compassion for her grandfather made her more open to other people's suffering."

"I don't understand what you're getting at Robert."

"There's a lot we don't understand sir, but I'm telling you I believe what is troubling that lass in not of this world.

CHAPTER TWENTY-THREE

Vincent Strickland stood atop the dune looking out over the lake. The frothy white peaks of cresting waves that rolled into shore accenting the surreal quality of the scene before him. The lake was a blue grey of the most beautiful and ethereal hue. If he wasn't seeing it himself, he would not believe it possible for the lake and sky to melt into each other like this. Perhaps there was a God, Vincent thought. Perhaps he had been wrong all these years and Madison had been right.

Vincent dropped down on one knee in the sand on the overlook. He wanted to say a prayer, but his mind instead was filled with roiling waves of doubt, coupled with the music of Madison's voice and the prayer was in a misty place waiting to be born. He could not forgive himself for what he'd done. He remembered Madison asking where he learned to hate himself so much. He believed it was the day he realized he would not be good enough for her, because she was too good. And that's what made his brain burn right now, because he loved her. He had caused her pain and he knew he was going to hell, yet her words kept ringing in his mind like small bells that gave him hope. Apparently there were new rules about heaven and hell. And Madison had been ready to set his world straight that day in the restaurant. God's Divine Mercy is what she had called it. Well he wasn't about to become religious for anyone, but he was starting to respect her views.

He was truly sorry for what he'd done to her paintings. They were really nothing compared to how much they meant to her. And there was no one in her life now except her aunt after Nick had died. The aunt was getting old. Who would Madison have when her aunt was gone? He would always be there for her, if she would only let him.

Vincent reached into his vehicle and pulled out a pack of cigarettes. There was only one left. He thrust it into his mouth. His hand shook as he lit a match. He watched the wind blow the match out and tried again while leaning into the open car window. He took a drag off the cigarette, quickly smoking half of it before flicking it on the ground and stomping on the butt. Sliding back into his car, he tossed the empty pack out the window.

It was so easy to have people believe you were abused, he thought. *Oliver Whitestone had only tried to help him! He had betrayed both Madison and Oliver!* Self hatred burned inside Vincent's brain like a smoldering coal as he put the car in gear and drove to the hospital to the only person that could put out that fire.

THE REVERAND LUCY CLAREMONT SAT IN A CHAIR in the waiting room of the hospital. She was a spry woman in her eighties with white hair and a round face that showed very little in the way of wrinkles. Apparently there was a young woman in a coma-like condition and a friend of hers by the name of Robert McDuff had asked her to help figure out the cause of the young woman's illness as she had done with several other similar cases in her lifetime.

When Lucy first went into the young woman's room at the hospital, she sensed immediately that there was much more going on than she anticipated. There was no way to describe the depth of sorrow she found. For a good hour, she sat quietly connecting with the energy that seemed to consume her, trying desperately to find a fragment of Madison's soul that was not drowning in it. Now she sat in the waiting room in an effort to clear her mind and emotions before she went back to resume her vigil at Madison's bedside. Finally feeling strong enough to take up the challenge once again, a challenge she was certain God had given her, Lucy made her way down the hall past the nurses' station, praying that she would be able to locate a spark of the woman's light to bring her up out of the darkness.

Lucy braced herself mentally and emotionally as she walked into the hospital room again. She struggled to maintain her composure as she experienced a sudden jolt to her senses that was utterly draining. Sitting down quietly on the chair in the corner, she again got the undeniable impression that Madison Andrews was at the bottom of a very black and dangerous well. And something was filling that well up, only it wasn't water, it was energy that held so much despair and sorrow that it was keeping Madison anchored in a hellish place almost like riptide that was not allowing her to surface. This energy, Lucy sensed, was determined to hang on to her pulling her down with it. If, Lucy deduced, she could get past the tide of energy and locate a glimmer of Madison's spirit, then perhaps she had a chance to nudge the young woman psychically and bring her consciousness up to another level where they could hope to reach her.

Lucy was contemplating this when a young man walked into the hospital room. He didn't notice her at first, but went directly to the bed where Madison lay. She noticed his eyes were glazed and he was reeking of cigarette smoke. For several minutes, Lucy was certain she sensed a ray of light in the darkness where Madison was held captive. It was like a small spark trying to take flight. As the young man stood looking down over the young woman's body, Lucy was certain she glimpsed a trace of Madison's spirit piercing the negative energy and reaching up through the riptide to him. For several minutes she was certain that Madison was reaching out to the young man, but then without warning, a snap of resistant energy shut Madison down and propelled her into the well again.

Lucy felt nauseated. What was Madison fighting against? It was not her own emotions that were keeping her captive, but rather, something foreign, an entity with a personality quite different from Madison's. Was this entity trying to do her harm?

Just then another man who appeared to her to be in his late thirties walked into the room. For a moment Lucy thought there was going to be an outburst from the younger man as he turned abruptly, quite startled by the second man's presence. For several seconds both men stared at each other, neither of them saying anything, until someone did speak, and Lucy realized with a good amount of surprise and relief that it was Madison who spoke out in a weak voice.

Both men turned to the bed in surprise. The older man went to her, while the younger man stood transfixed. "What did she say?" the younger man finally turned and asked Lucy, his eyes questioning and bloodshot.

Lucy remembered that the older man leaning over Madison must be Collin, the psychologist. She had never met him before, but Wanda had described him and told her he might visit. But who was the younger man?

Vincent looked at Lucy and then at Collin. "Will she be alright?"

"Why don't you say something to her? Perhaps we'll get a reaction again," Collin said, leaning over Madison.

Vincent nodded. Taking a few steps forward, he also leaned over the bed and whispered something near Madison's ear.

Madison's expressionless face gathered into a painful grimace. She began to thrash around. Collin could see she was on the verge of pulling out her IV. Quickly, Collin pushed the call button to summon a nurse. Just as one of the RN's walked into the room, Madison went limp again.

The nurse quickly pulled the curtains around Madison's bed. "I would like everyone to leave the room for a few minutes while I check the machines and do a few other tests on the patient," she announced with a comforting smile. You can wait in the patient lounge. I'll send someone in to tell you when you can come back.

WANDA WAS ECSTATIC WHEN SHE FOUND out Madison had spoken. "Thank you, Lucy!" Wanda said embracing the older woman. "I've been praying all afternoon. It appears my prayers have been answered!"

Lucy gave Wanda an encouraging smile. "It really wasn't only me, although I would like to think it was. It was Vincent's presence that prompted her to speak."

"Vincent? Is that someone who works at the hospital?"

"I tried to talk to him, but he seemed to be in a hurry to leave. I heard him tell the nurse, when he first came in, that he was Madison's cousin. He looked extremely shaken when he saw

Madison. He left without talking to anyone." Lucy frowned.

"We don't have any other family in this area. It's only Madison and I now after her husband died. There is some extended family, but they are across the country. I wonder who Vincent is? What did Collin say about all this? He's the psychologist I told you about. Did he talk to you?"

"He really didn't say anything. He left in quite a hurry afterwards too." Lucy took a deep breath. "Wanda there is one more thing. I did sense something that I think you need to know that may affect Madison in some way in the future, that is, if and when she comes out of this. I believe both Vincent and Collin are in love with her."

COLLIN FOUND MADISON'S NOTEBOOK when he returned to his home. His mind was buzzing with the hope that she would be alright. There had been a big change in her today. He had to admit, as skeptical as he was, he felt Lucy being there with her had made the difference in her crying out, if only to facilitate the episode. Yet he felt it was really Vincent's presence that had caused Madison to speak. Who was this Vincent? Sitting down at the kitchen table he began to reread the story Madison had written. Afterwards he leafed through the notebook and read several pages again.

Ananda had made it a point to be kind to the young boy in every way possible. She knew she would miss him after she left for Detroit. But of course he would still be able to slide down the dunes and watch the lake glow at sunset like they had always done together. She would be stuck in stuffy St. Mary's girl's school, thoughts of plump bass and minnows on her mind. Father might as well have stuck her in a convent, there would be no hikes for her or warm caressing sun. Detroit was a stuffy city and she'd probably die before she turned fourteen.

With a frown on her face, Ananda got up abruptly. "John," she said, surveying the sky, "the sun will set soon, and we have a long ways to go through the woods, I don't want Father angry again. We better get going now."

.

The poem he found was on the next to last page. Had she written it for her husband?

> I see you crying,
> I wonder how my touch
> Can soothe your heart,
> White shows so much.
> Against dark.
> How can I kiss you
> Without them frowning at me?
> And having them hate
> Before they can see?

Collin retrieved his cell phone and looked up the number of the historical society. He planned to call the museum in the morning.

MARGARET WICKERS FROWNED. She was a stout woman in her late sixties with short black hair streaked with gray. Collin stared at the handwriting in the journal where Edna's plump finger pointed. He shook his head.

"Thanks for helping me find these."

"You're welcome. What did you say you were writing again?"

Deep in thought, Collin turned to leave without answering and gave Margaret a slight wave. He walked quickly down the steps of the museum to the parking lot, and noticed Robert McDuff sitting in his car reading a newspaper. He waved when Robert lifted his eyes for a moment and looked his way. Robert rolled down his window.

"It looks like yer havin' the same ideas I am." Robert called through the open window.

Collin walked up to his car. "What do you mean, Robert?"

"Are you reading those journals Madison was looking at the day she collapsed in her bedroom? She was here at the museum before she went to the hospital, you know. Wanda found out about it from her landlady Anna. She was doing research for the story she's been writing."

"I read several journals kept by a priest," Collin said." I believe they are what Madison read, Robert. It looks like she was using the information as a basis for the story. She was certainly inspired by the shipwreck that she had found."

"Aye, she definitely was. It's funny how she took up writing so suddenly when it seems the only thing that really interested her at all was her art throughout her life. I do find that very interesting, indeed. Wanda thought it was interesting too. "

"She was very compelled to write the story. I agree with that," Collin said studying Robert's face. "Does something trouble you about that?"

"The idea that she's in a coma right now does trouble me sir and the fact that they don't know what's causing it."

"It definitely troubles me too. I'm not at liberty to tell you anything Madison said in therapy, but I can assure you she had a very frightening moment in the water near the shipwreck. Perhaps writing was her way of coming to grips with whatever has been troubling her."

"Or perhaps someone is compelling her to tell this particular story for some reason."

"What do you mean?"

"I'd say we need to call a meeting on this, sir, and put our heads together. Maybe Lucy has some ideas to how we can help Madison, Mr. Richardson."

"HEAVEN IS REAL," Lucy said. "And it's more beautiful than you can imagine. I actually went through the tunnel myself."

"You never told me that, Lucy." Robert said.

"It was a long time ago, Robert. It happened when I was a child. Since then I've always wanted to share what I saw with everyone. People think me a little strange at times I must say. What happened to you, Lucy? How did you die?"

"When I was a girl, I fell through the ice while skating. Fortunately my father who was a physician at the time was with me. He pulled me out and gave me CPR. Because the water was close to freezing I didn't have any brain damage. I told my father what I saw, that I had started to go through a tunnel and had seen my grandmother who had recently died standing in a very bright light holding her hands out to me. Behind her I could see a beautiful color filled sky with magnificent shining clouds floating above. I was drawn to my beloved grandmother's presence and so wanted to feel her arms around me again. But apparently it wasn't my time to go and suddenly I was brought back into the cold with the wind howling about my face and my father leaning over me. I was shivering My father had tears streaming down his face. He said he believed me and told me afterwards some of his patients had near death experiences just like mine.

"I'm glad he believed you. Of course people still went to church back then and that helped them believe in heaven." Wanda said. "Many people think going to church is unnecessary these days."

"I think people question religion because very often it creates frightening scenarios for children when they shouldn't have anything to fear, Wanda," Collin said. He took out his cell phone and glanced at the time. It was exactly noon. The doctors told them it would be at least another hour before they would have any news on Madison.

"Churches are definitely needed, like my church," Lucy began, "but I wish more churches would focus on love, compassion and forgiveness, not damnation. The truth is God is pure love. He is a God of infinite mercy and we are all his children on this planet. We need only seek him and we are on our way to his world of hope and grace."

"Someone once said 'the grace we find in each other is God. I think it was Richard Paul Evans," Wanda looked at the clock in the cafeteria and then closed her eyes for a moment. "Did you know Saint John Paul II didn't believe in an actual hell? He believed hell was not a physical place, but rather a state of consciousness that people attained when they rejected the goodness of God."

"I find many people put themselves in hell when they're still alive, because of the terrible decisions they make." Collin said.

"Or people are put through hell because of the actions of others," Robert added. "I have seen many a suffering person during my years of work that have been victims of crimes."

"Speaking of unfortunate souls," Collin looked up from his cell phone. "I believe the woman that Madison has been writing about is Ananda Kettering. She was doing research on the shipwreck we found in the water near Eagle Bay that Ananda was on board when she died. Apparently the young woman was left on the ship in the mizzen mast when it foundered. Whether it was by accident or on purpose no one really knows.

Wanda winced. "From how Madison described it in her story, the woman was tied to the mast and hung there almost like she was crucified."

Robert shook his head. "Now that is indeed a picture to ponder." He paused, deep in thought for a moment. "Wanda I talked to one of the nurse's today. Madison has cried out several times asking for *bitter waters*. Does anyone know what that could possibly mean?"

"Madison became agitated in the hospital and called it out several times. It's as though she's in another world and she's trying to get out, to come home, but something won't let her, Robert!"

"Or someone." Lucy said softly.

Wanda shook her head. "Madison was always such a sensitive compassionate child. It's just so wrong that this is happening to her!"

Lucy placed her hand over Wanda's hand. "Sometimes the most sensitive people suffer the most on this earth, Wanda. We must be there for them." She paused and took a deep breath. "Wanda I am certain the truth in all of this is that the woman Collin mentioned, who was left on the schooner to drown, was so traumatized by the way she died that her spirit is still attached to the earth. This woman latched onto Madison when she went near the wreckage like a drowning person struggling to stay afloat."

CHAPTER TWENTY FOUR

Oliver Whitestone looked out the window of his art studio. His eyes swept the lines of the meadow behind his cottage and rested on a group of maple trees his grandfather had planted when he was a boy. Over a decade ago, when his mother had died, he and his uncle had spread her ashes beneath the maples, mixing her remains with the rich dark soil that carpeted the ground beneath them.

"Rest in peace Mother," Oliver whispered. He turned from the window and strolled back to his desk. Sitting down in the large overstuffed chair, he took a deep breath and glanced at the sculpture he had just finished that morning. It was of a Native American woman with a wolf lying at her feet. It reminded him of Madison Andrews.

Oliver pulled out his cell phone. He brought up the number of the Northern Cross and hesitated for a moment before calling. Finally he hit the button.

An older woman answered the phone.

"Madison is not here right now, Oliver."

"Could I leave her a message?"

"She's in the hospital."

"Is she still sick?"

"The doctors don't know for certain what's causing Madison's problem. I wish I could tell you more."

"Please let me know if there's anything I can do."

"Thank you, Oliver," Wanda took a breath. "How is your foundation going?"

"The Skyward Foundation is doing well. Thanks for asking. We appreciate the donations Madison has made for the children."

"It's certainly our pleasure, Oliver."

"Before you go, I have a question for you. Did you or Madison find a small leather pouch in the gallery? I might have dropped it when I was there the last time I brought in some of my artwork."

"Wanda let out a breath. "Did you say a leather pouch? I have something in the safe. I'll call you right back."

When Wanda called him back five minutes later she could hear the relief in Oliver's voice. "It's quite a beautiful little piece of work," she said as she fingered the beads on the worn leather. "It must be very old."

"It was my great grandmother's. It's something that has been in my family for over a century."

"I'll keep it here at the store for you until you come in," Wanda's voice broke a little, "but Madison won't be here of course. Please excuse me," she said trying to regain her composure. "Will you bring in more of your sculptures? I have people asking for them."

"I do have one. I'll bring it with me," he told her before hanging up.

FOR SEVERAL MOMENTS WANDA THOUGHT SHE WAS HAVING A STROKE. Her ears were ringing. There was also a buzzing sound. Feeling light headed, she set the leather pouch down on the counter in the art gallery. The sound in her ears stopped immediately. She picked the pouch up again. This time besides the buzzing in her ears she felt nauseated. *Was she getting sick?*

She glanced at the clock on the wall. It was five minutes to four. Madison usually closed the store at six, but for some reason she was feeling exhausted right now. She decided to close early. *It would do no good if she wound up in the hospital with Madison!* The thought brought tears to her eyes. She prayed the good Lord would allow the girl to get over this, whatever *this* was and to live her life in peace. Wanda shivered. *Could Lucy possibly be right?*

The Catholic Church certainly believed in possession. She'd read numerous accounts of actual possessions that were written by a priest by the name of Father Gabrielle who was now the head exorcist for the Vatican. He claimed to have performed over 70,000 exorcisms throughout his life. One question after another filled her head. When she returned to her condo, she decided to say her prayers to calm her racing mind. Afterwards she slipped into her bedroom to lie down. The ticking of the clock on the bedside table soothed her and she fell into a deep sleep.

Slipping deeply into a dream that felt more real than anything she had ever imagined before, she found herself lying on another bed in another room that was unfamiliar to her. Wanda knew immediately she was in someone else's body and was about to give birth to a baby as she looked upon the round protruding mound of a stomach that was not hers. Almost immediately she felt the stomach tighten. She was caught by surprise as the pain ripped through her. The woman standing beside her bed in the dream, a nurse or midwife, dressed in blue, gave her a rolled up wash cloth to put in her mouth. It was wet and cold.

"Here bite down on this, my darling," she said.

The pains were coming faster and faster. Wanda could feel the pressure surging through her as the labor picked up momentum.

Lord Jesus, something was wrong! Was it supposed to feel this way?

"I must have my mother!" she heard herself cry out.

"Unfortunately your mother is not here, my dear child. If you would have listened to her, you would not be in this predicament, the nurse said not unkindly. Quickly the woman switched her position by the bedside and stood between Wanda's legs. "You need to push now!"

The pressure that had been building inside grew stronger and stronger as the pains climaxed and then suddenly she felt the baby being expelled from her body.

Relieved that the pain had finally subsided, she lay back on her pillow and waited for what seemed like an eternity for the midwife to finish what she was doing and place the baby in her arms. Suddenly she heard voices. She realized someone else had entered the room. They left quickly. Unable to be patient any longer, she asked with a tired raspy voice, "Please tell me, if it was a boy or girl."

It was stillborn," the midwife, or whoever she was, simply said.

Wanda almost choked on the sorrow that welled up inside of her as the words echoed in her mind and she discerned their meaning. The baby had died!

"Wait." she cried out. "I want to see my baby!"

"We cannot allow it now, the nurse said not unkindly. It will traumatize you."

"Was it a boy or a girl?" Wanda felt tears streaming down her face.

"It was a little girl," the nurse said. She handed her a washcloth to wipe her face.

Suddenly Wanda turned and saw something sitting on the little table next to her. She reached for it and held it out to the woman. "Please make sure this is put with her body."

The nurse took little bag. "What is it "

Wanda smiled sadly through her tears. Please keep it with her body so she so she has something to remind her of how much she was loved while she's waiting for me in heaven."

"The baby is certainly not in heaven," the nurse said quietly, "she wasn't baptized."

Wanda let out an enormous sob at the nurse's words. Tears poured down her cheeks. They tasted salty and bitter. She thought her heart would burst.

WANDA'S EYES FLEW OPEN with a start. She was shaking from head to toe.

Without hesitation, she called Oliver Whitestone.

"My grandmother told us that her mother died soon after giving birth to her. She stayed in Chicago, at the orphanage, almost all of her young life until she was adopted."

"Oliver, what was your great grandmother's name?"

"Mary Smith. They told her at the orphanage that Mary had been a young woman who was destitute and had no family."

"What do you know about the pouch?"

"My grandmother was told at the orphanage that her mother had wanted her to have it. It was surprising that the nurses kept it for her all those years."

"But why would she give her baby something like that? What

157

meaning did it have to her?"

"We always believed it was some sort of *talisman* or *fetish* used to keep away evil spirits."

"AS I TOLD YOU ON THE PHONE, I felt very strange after handling the pouch," Wanda said as she poured a cup of coffee for Lucy Claremont. "My ears started ringing and then they were buzzing, Lucy. Then I felt sick to my stomach. After that I became extremely tired, so tired in fact I had to lie down for a while. I then had the most intense dream about giving birth."

Lucy looked up from the notebook that was sitting open on the table in front of her. "I want to write this all down, Wanda," she said, holding a pen in her hand. "I'm trying to keep a detailed history of what we know so we don't forget anything. I believe it will help us a great deal."

Wanda took a sip of her own coffee and glanced at Lucy's notebook. When she looked up again she could see several customers entering the store. Thankfully one of the women Madison had hired to help at the gallery was in today. Jessica greeted the customers and then nodded at Wanda who could see her through the open door of the art room.

Lucy pursed her lips. "Going back to your experience with the leather bag, my guess is that you were picking up energy from it. Did you know that in the eighteen hundreds, a man by the name of Joseph Buchanan came up with the idea that all things give off vibrations. What's interesting is that Rhodes believed the past could be unearthed through what he called lpsychometry as readily as an archeologist could reveal ancient truths."

"This is all new to me, Lucy. Will I get ill touching it again?"

"If it makes you feel better, I'll handle it. I think the pouch may have acted as a sort of conduit and played a part in Madison's condition." Lucy pursed her lips again. "From what you told me about your conversation with Oliver, I am very prone to believe they lied to his grandmother about her mother dying soon after giving birth. I also believe Mary Smith was not the woman's real name. They apparently were trying to hide the fact that Oliver's great grandmother was pregnant. I believe she may have been sent away to have the baby. To a home for unwed mothers."

"So you think the young woman I dreamt about is Oliver's

great grandmother?"

"I believe very strongly it possibly is. I also believe Oliver's great grandmother was or is Ananda Kettering."

"I'll be back in a moment." Wanda turned and headed to the gallery office. Minutes later she returned with Oliver's leather bag and handed it to Lucy.

Lucy held the pouch in her hand. Her eyes suddenly grew wide.

"What is it Lucy?"

"There are so many images jumbled together! It's as though I'm watching a movie in fast forward."

Lucy carefully opened the bag and looked inside. She pulled out several objects one by one. She placed a small cross, a tiny shell, a wooden bead, and a small ring on the table in front of her. Peering into the bag again, she gently pulled out a piece of fabric and placed it next to the other tiny objects. After looking them over Lucy slid the tiny shell into the palm of her hand. She closed her eyes for several moments. Suddenly they popped open. "I saw a boy and a girl! They were on a beach. It was a stormy day and they were holding each other and crying. I could see the dark clouds gathering in the sky above them! "

Very carefully Lucy set the shell down and picked up the small cross that looked like it had been part of a rosary. Once again she held the object in the palm of her hand and closed her eyes. "I can feel the blessing here. It is instilled with much love." Her eyes sparkled when she looked at Wanda.

Hesitating for a moment, she looked over the other objects, finally she put the small cross down and picked up the wooden bead. She held it between her fingers. A look of surprise and wonder spread over her face, then her face set in a frown.

"I saw a woman! She was in a small cabin in the woods. It was snowing. She was very cold. I could actually feel her hunger. She was holding a baby. I could hear the baby crying. I heard the woman say *bitter waters,* as she tried to comfort the baby!"

Wanda's eyes also grew wide. "What do you suppose it could mean?"

"I wish I knew!"

"A woman with a baby in her arms? It could not have been Oliver's great grandmother then." Wanda shook her head. "Ananda

Kettering would never have held her child. In my dream they took the baby away before she had seen it, telling her it was stillborn. Who could this woman you saw possibly be?"

"That is the million dollar question," Lucy exclaimed. "I clearly heard the woman say the words *bitter waters* over and over as she held the crying baby. I'm sure *nibi* is the word for water!"

"Was it a warning?"

"It appears to me *bitter waters* could be some kind of warning," Lucy once again grasped the bead between her thumb and forefinger and closed her eyes again."

"Sweet Jesus!" Wanda exclaimed. "We have been forgetting that Madison has been calling out those words in the hospital! And I dreamt about two young children only several days ago!"

CHAPTER TWENTY FIVE

The first thing he noticed when the alarm went off unexpectedly at three a.m. was that the bedroom was ice cold. Wincing, Collin hit the snooze button and fell back onto his pillow. Instantly, he felt warm moist air on his arm and the sound of heavy breathing by his ear. When he turned his head there were two large eyes peering at him from the shadows near his face. He switched on his lamp and ran his hand over Goliath's nose. The dog whimpered.

"Don't tell me you need to go out again. I just let you out before we went to sleep."

The dog gave a quick bark. Collin yanked himself out of bed and threw his coat on over his sweat pants. He grabbed his shoes and slipped them on before he headed out the door with Goliath.

When he got outside he studied the full moon as he walked Goliath to the park. Filling his nostrils with the musty aroma of fallen leaves, he made his way across the street to the park on the waterfront. After taking care of dog, he sat down on a bench overlooking the bay. The water was lit with a silvery beam of light from the moon's reflection that looked liked a walkway. For several minutes he sat gazing up at the night sky not noticing the lone figure that appeared out of the shadows beside him, until the man spoke.

"Ah we meet again," Robert McDuff said. "May I?" His hand hovered over Goliath's head.

"Be my guest, as long as it's okay with Goliath, it's fine with me."

After petting the dog, Robert sat down next to Collin on the bench.

"What brings you out at this late hour, Robert?"

"I couldn't sleep my friend. I've been thinking of Madison, of course. Both Lucy and myself believe if we can find out what the words she has been calling out in the hospital mean we'll be able to help her,"

Collin shifted position to face him. "Wanda called me tonight and told me what happened."

"Did she tell you about the vision Lucy had. She believes the words *bitter waters* may be the key to understanding what is troubling our spirit."

"Our spirit?"

"The ghost that is haunting Madison and keeping her in that godforsaken place sir, that's what I'm talking about."

"I looked up those words when she first said them, Robert. And I came across a book that was called *Bitter Waters*. It was about the Soviet Union. Close to two million Poles were sent to the frozen hell of Siberia because of Stalin. It all leads me to believe that Madison is exhibiting generational post traumatic stress, besides dealing with an enormous amount of grief which is causing her to sink into a state of some sort of catatonia, which resembles a coma."

"Please sir, I know I'm Scottish, but simple English would do very well here."

"I believe Madison has been traumatized, Robert. I believe she was very close to her grandfather and took on his memories and his pain as many children of survivors do after her parents died. She's suffering from what is called generational post traumatic stress as is every child from every war torn country whether they experienced a war first hand or not. It boils down to what happened to their family, to the trauma they experienced. So to put it more simply for you, there is definitely a psychological cause to Madison's coma. Now I know I may have broken doctor-patient confidentiality with that statement. So if you'll excuse me I should perhaps leave before I say anymore."

"You need not say more, but again please hear me out for Madison's sake." Robert pulled a cigar out of his pocket and stuck it in his mouth. "Is it not a true scientific fact that energy can never be destroyed, that it changes forms? To that end we must believe that at death we may lose our bodies, but we keep the souls we've created in our lives. Do you know, sir, that many parapsychologists say the soul continues to have the same habits, thoughts, memories, feelings and most of all flaws as it had existing in the physical plane. So think of the tremendous shock when someone dies unexpectedly and enters the spirit world like the woman who died on board the schooner did. I believe and so does Lucy that the woman is still in a state of panic and terror because of the ordeal she was going through at the time of her death. At this point, sir, she's doing what comes naturally to a person who is drowning, the spirit is holding on for dear life, so to speak, to the nearest source of rescue and that is Madison. I've studied possession, being an amateur parapsychologist myself. I must say people who are possessed who fall into trance states like Madison can become very ill."

"So how do you think we can help this ghost?"

"The woman doesn't know she's dead. We need to help her realize that important fact so she can leave this earth plane, and find peace. She is caught in a cycle of fear, sir. And that fear is keeping her in this dimension. She's clinging to Madison for dear life. The only problem of course is that she's dead. There is also another thing. I believe this woman lost a child and needs to know her child is safe. Besides saying "bitter waters" over and over, Madison has also called out for someone by the name of John."

"I presume from what I've read in Madison's story that John was the woman's lover?"

Robert nodded. "We believe the young woman was going home to be with him when she died on board the schooner. Lucy said she saw images that suggest the young woman had been sent away to give birth to his baby and was coming home when the schooner foundered and she drowned.

"It's a wonderful story, Robert. But how could it possibly be true?"

"It is indeed true, if you read the journals kept by the priest. And there are more of them on South Manitou Island that were just found recently. They are at the small museum there. There has to be more information in them that could help us find the key to helping Madison and the spirit. I'm afraid, however, that they can't be taken off the island. They are owned by the National Park. So someone must go to them."

"Robert, I would imagine there would be some evidence in the journals that could possibly confirm your beliefs, some evidence that Madison couldn't possibly have known that she cited in her writing.

"My man, she has called out the name, *John,* on several occasions, besides saying those particular words."

"Yes, and Madison has also been involved in doing research on her grandfather's history. *Bitter Waters*, as I said before, is the title of a book on the Soviet Union. To me, her calling out those words would make a case for her being affected by that history."

THE BOAT WAS DEAD IN THE WATER. Once more Collin tried the engine. There was only a clicking sound when he turned the key. He looked around the lake. There were no other boats in sight. If he needed a tow he would have to call Jim Tucker and hope for the best. At least he had picked a good day to get stuck. The temperature was in the low seventies. For this time of the year, the weather was miraculous; the sun was shining without a cloud in the sky.

Taking a deep breath, he let it out, focusing on his destination. It would more than likely take him an hour to get there. If he got the engine started. Wincing he grabbed his cell phone and dialed his friend Jim Tucker, the owner of the old Sea Ray he'd borrowed. He was thankful he got a signal.

"Jim, this boat of yours conked out on me and I can't get it started. Any suggestions?"

Jim Tuckers voice cut in and out as Collin tried to decipher what he was saying.

Finally, Collin opened the engine compartment and looked inside. It took a few minutes of adjustments, but the motor started right up as Jim said it would.

The rest of the ride went without a hitch. When they got within a few miles of their destination he let Goliath out of the cabin. The giant dog yawned and stretched, then wagged his tail when he walked out on the deck.

"Big help you are," Collin said as he glanced at Goliath who sat down next to him while he drove.

When he got to the island, Collin docked the boat quickly. If he hurried to the information center he might make it home before the sun set. If not, he was prepared to spend the night in the small marina. Robert had told him the journals they were looking for were kept in the museum among other material that had been written more than a century and a half before. He was also told Julie Taylor was the ranger on duty today. Thankfully Margaret Wickers had talked to her on the phone and convinced her to help locate the diaries for him.

Robert and Lucy believed Madison was being haunted by a spirit. He shook his head. Many people around the world still believed in possession when in fact there was some type of psychological disorder in the afflicted person. He knew he would do anything to help Madison. If that included exorcizing a ghost, well he knew his father would approve. The only thing was, the ghosts they were dealing with could be any number of issues that were affecting her psyche.

JULIE TAYLOR LED HIM into the back room of the small building the park used for exhibits. She climbed onto a stool and brought down a box. She took out several small books that were covered with dusty black cloth that was fraying at the edges.

"Be careful with them," she said, handing them to Collin. They're very old. We stored them in here until we can have someone from the main office look at them. You're very lucky that they're still here. I would normally have you put on gloves to look at them, so please, like I said, be very gentle with them. The priest's handwriting is hard to decipher, but the housekeeper, Eliza Strong's is readable. If you need me I'll be in the main building."

Julie left him in the room with the light on. Seconds later her head appeared in the doorway again. "When you're done just leave them on the table and I'll put them away, she added."

"Thanks Julie, I appreciate it."

Collin sat down on a wooden chair that was placed next to a small table and pulled out the notebooks he had brought along in his backpack; one of them was Madison's and one of them was his own. He looked outside for a moment through the weathered panes of glass that separated him from the natural beauty of the island then down at the diaries that lay on the table in front of him.

CHAPTER TWENTY SIX

I hope whoever finds these journals will forgive me for being such a coward, but I am afraid to go to the authorities. Men with money and power like him have always frightened me. I very much believe it was because of him that Ananda Kettering was left in the rigging to die on board that schooner when it foundered. I heard some of the crewmen talking about what they'd seen. I believe it would do no good for me to speak up anyway. Everyone would surely believe what I said about him, but no one would have the courage to do anything.

Don't get me wrong, I don't think he is the worst man who ever walked the face of the earth. I know there are others worse. He's done a great deal for this town. but I do think all his money has gone to his head. Nathanial Burgess thinks he can have anything he wants and that includes women which of course is the way of the world for females it seems.

The whole thing is so sad, Ananda being left on board the ship to drown and that poor Indian woman, Blue Goose winding up with Nathanial's baby living out in the woods and almost freezing to death so many years before. How Nathanial used Blue Goose then left her with child to freeze in the cold was such an abomination. It certainly broke my heart to pieces seeing her in that old cabin with the wind howling outside and her crying baby hanging on her hip when I came to bring her food. She always looked so thin and run down. It was odd how she called the child "bitter waters," in Indian which is a strange name, I know, but Father told me it was because of the baby's tears which made sense if you thought about it. If not for Father she and the baby would have starved or froze or both all those years.

Bless Father he was always there for everyone. He never complained about his own troubles. People didn't know how much he suffered doing the Lord's work. When he came upon Blue Goose tying a rope around her neck trying to kill herself he helped her down from that stool she had climbed upon, and blessed her, sending those demons out of her. Afterwards he found a warm place for her to stay. He placed the baby with two good people until Blue Goose was well enough to raise it on her own. The boy grew up to be a fine one too. He learned how to read the good book from cover to cover as he grew. And to honor his mother. I found out Blue Goose had named him John Baptiste because she had asked Father for the baptism to ward off the evil spirits in that baby's little body so the crying would stop. Let me tell you Father had been pleased with the name. Well John's crying finally did stop forever that day the ship was sinking. It was the same day he'd found out what the lumberman had done to his wife.

It was such a shame all that transpired. Father had secretly married them two young people when he found out they were planning to run away because Ananda had gotten pregnant. It was after Ananda came back from Detroit and the girl's school the doctor had sent her to. Father always knew what was going on between the two of them. He knew that they had loved each other since they were children.

The men were cruel to John because they knew how much Ananda cared for him, him being part Indian, a half breed. The women in town thought he was one of the finest they had seen. I heard them talk about him when they came to church. Being the priest's housekeeper and all I always heard things when the congregation would be leaving the church after mass. It was a small group to be sure, not a lot of Catholics in the area. But the few that came were certainly devout and loved their faith like me. It was the faith that saved John Baptiste from a pitiful life. I do not doubt that he would have been a far different one if he had not had Father Chabert in his life guiding him on the rights and wrongs of the world. So now it is up to me to let the world know what happened. I believe dear Ananda deserves that much in her name and so does John Baptiste and Father Chabert The three of them did not deserve to die such deaths, but rather to have their names mean such a thing as the world will love and respect,

Sincerely and Respectfully
Eliza Strong

Collin looked up from Eliza's journal. Taking a deep breath he glanced out the window. *So the baby had been named Bitter Waters!* Madison had called out those words several times when he was in her room at the hospital! He pulled out his notebook and reread his notes. *Wasn't Nathanial Burgess the lumberman Madison had mentioned in therapy? She had talked about a painting that her friend Eden was planning to display of her great grandfather. He had been the founder of Eagle Bay!*

He let out a whistle. "Very interesting!"

He scanned the rest of Eliza's diary. It was filled with entries describing her life as Father Chabert's housekeeper. At the back of the journal, he came across an envelope that was folded in half. He carefully extracted the piece of paper inside and read it. He let out a gasp. Quickly he found his backpack and Madison's blue spiral notebook. He flipped them both open on the table. His heart picked up speed. *How could Madison have possibly known about the poem?* Julie Taylor had told him the journals had been discovered several weeks earlier under the floor boards of one of the old cabins on the island that was being excavated and restored by the National Park Service. He was one of the first to see them besides the rangers. They had never been on display or seen by the public.

He took a deep breath and let it out. *There was no denying there was something remarkable going on!* He shook his head. He was still of the opinion that some of the so called "ghosts" that were affecting Madison were linked to her grandfather. From day one in therapy he'd been concerned about how much her grandfather's history had affected her life. He'd been more than a little impressed and relieved when she'd told him about the project she'd started with her husband, *The Garden of Light Project* was what she called it. They'd raised enough money to buy a small farm in Poland and had planned on developing the land into a peace park before Nick's cancer diagnosis. Instead of focusing on her grandfather's past Madison had told him she'd found the perfect way to focus on the future, and yet pay homage to the victims of so many horrible wars throughout the ages. Her dream had given her a sense of happiness that she'd not felt in her entire life . . . that is until her husband died.

He flipped through the pages in the notebook again and read the entries she had made about her trip to Europe and her inspiration for the peace park.

The camp was permeated with sadness. I remember seeing an old man sitting on the steps of one of the barracks. He must have been a survivor because he was leaning forward with his head in his hands sobbing. That memory will always haunt me. My roommate and I walked through the camp surveying the buildings that day not believing the heartless conditions. The knowledge that my grandfather had been one of the prisoners there was devastating to me and I almost couldn't breathe. But my roommate and I had come up with a plan the night before. It was a small plan but the seeds we planted that afternoon grew inside me. And as time progressed, I could feel the vision healing me.

Wendy's ring had been inscribed with the words, faith, hope, and love inside. The ring I had brought along had been a plain silver band with a peace sign on it. We slipped away from the tour group for a few moments and found a spot near the railroad tracks where the prisoners were unloaded to bury them. It was under one of the ties near a guard platform.

It was such a gloomy overcast day, and I couldn't believe at first that I was standing in this sad place. That afternoon I felt like I was literally planting the seeds of faith, hope and love in the earth. When we came back from the tour and I was finally at home, those words took root in me and for the first time I didn't see the ugliness of the camp and the horror where so many innocent people had died, but rather I focused on the rings that we had planted. I envisioned a place where people from all over the world could go to pray for peace and create a place of beauty and healing.

He remembered very vividly how Madison had looked sitting in his office the afternoon she told him about the project.

Collin gazed out the window again and caught a glimpse of the waning light being filtered through the trees. The slanting rays punctuated the shadows and lit up the ground below.

He knew Madison had been determined to find the beauty and goodness in the world when she could've been filled with bitterness. She was sensitive and kind. If she had one fault at all it was that she was too trusting.

He felt tears gather in his eyes. The afternoon she'd told him about the park, she'd also told him *Somewhere in Time* was her favorite movie. It was his favorite too. The film, with Christopher Reeve and Jane Seymour, had been shot on Mackinac Island at the Grand Hotel. It was about a playwright who traveled back in time to be with his one true love, the woman who spoke to his soul like no other. Madison had definitely touched his heart like no other woman he'd met. At that precise moment he felt like a time traveler who was lost in a dark murky dimension of space searching for a way to save the woman he loved!

Collin took a deep breath. He wiped away his tears. It had been over four months since he'd first met Madison Andrews on the beach near Eagle Bay. He'd gotten to know her inside and out in the many weeks he'd been treating her. He admired her courage and compassion. He admired her conviction and strength. Falling in love with a patient was something he never dreamed possible in his years of practice. And it was tearing him up inside. For the past several weeks he had not been sleeping. He was thinking about her Madison all the time. Besides being unethical it was unfair to her. She already told him about Vincent. How would he break this news to her. That is if she ever recovered. And if she did she needed someone who would not let his feelings get in the way of treating her properly.

He could see that the sun was getting low on the horizon; the sky was tinged with pink as the shadows of the descending night waited to take over. He thought of Goliath sitting on the boat. Fortunately, he had told Jim Tucker that he would spend the night on the island with Goliath if he needed to.

He looked down at the journal again. His throat grew tight. Very gently he picked up the yellowed paper that he'd retrieved out of the envelope and reread the poem, letting the words sink deep into his soul.

I see you crying
I wonder how much my touch
Can soothe your heart?
White shows so much
against dark.
How can I kiss you
without them frowning
at me?
And having them hate
before they can see.
They don't know
you feel pain;
that you bleed when you
are cut.
That the sun and sky are the same
to you as to them.
And raindrops do not turn to mud
as they touch your ears,
they are "color" blind to our tears.
You've given me a love that was soft,
a love I know was good.
Were flowers wrong to grow taller
where we stood?
Your tears were jewels against your dark skin.
They were a place to hide all our dreams and hopes in.

The poem was entitled Bitter Waters. The name Ananda was clearly written on the bottom of the page. It spoke of the undeniable heartache of two people who loved each other and had been kept apart. Madison had called out those very same words in the hospital. What was he to think now?

THE NEXT MORNING AFTER READING the rest of Eliza's journal he found the small cemetery where John Baptist had been buried on the island. Collin stood over the tombstone as the misty fall air swirled about him. He hoped it would get warmer and clearer as the day wore on. At the moment a flock of crows peered down at him with black beady eyes from maple trees that lined the cemetery while he shivered in the cold. The realization that he'd found Ananda's *beloved* filled Collin with sorrow and wonder. How on earth was it possible?

It had been quite astonishing to learn from Ms. Strong's diaries that John had been nineteen when he died after saving fourteen crewmen from a sinking ship. That ship had been the *Lydia,* the schooner Ananda Kettering had been on while returning from Chicago after having his baby. The schooner foundered in a storm near Eagle Bay. Ananda, who had been knocked unconscious, had been tied to the mizzen mast of the ship to prevent her from washing overboard. Hearing about a vessel in distress, the Life Saving Service had pulled their equipment twenty six miles by pony cart through treacherous weather to help in the rescue efforts. John Baptist had joined the rescuers, diving into the freezing waters again and again to get to his wife only to be stopped by the crewmen of the Lydia who were flailing around in the boiling lake calling out for help. In the end, Ananda's beloved John had brought all of fourteen men safely to shore before sadly falling victim himself to the bitter waters of a November gale.

Collin drew in a breath and let it out. It seemed the entire world had changed overnight. He could feel the cold air working its way into his bones as ominous gray clouds hung overhead. He glanced at the grave again and then at the path he'd taken through the woods. He'd hiked over five miles to get to the cemetery in the middle of the island. The thought of how frozen and fearful John must have been as he struggled in the icy waves while saving the crew of the foundering schooner, knowing his beloved Ananda was on the verge of death herself, filled Collin with sorrow. According to Eliza Strong, the young man had been a true hero; a hero who had been bullied and taunted by the very same men he had given his own life to save!

CHAPTER TWENTY SEVEN

The lake was choppy, filled with white caps that made the trip back to the mainland longer than he expected. When Collin pulled into the harbor in Leland, he tied up the Sea Ray and walked to the small canal by Fish Town. He bought a coffee at one of the few delis that remained open late in the season, and quickly drank the hot liquid to warm up. Afterwards he stopped at a gift shop named Reflections and bought a CD. It was classical piano music. It started to rain fifteen minutes into his drive back to Eagle Bay while he listened to Rick Lahman's rendition of Unchained Melody, and remembered how Madison had looked dancing to the song "Lady" by *Little River Band* at Belle's Tavern. At noon he stopped in Empire for lunch and had a cherry burger and fries. At one o'clock he called Wanda from the restaurant to see how Madison was and if there had been any changes.

He was surprised when Wanda told him she'd invited a sculptor that showed his work at Madison's gallery to the hospital that evening. Lucy Claremont was certain Oliver Whitestone's presence would help the spirit that was possessing Madison. Apparently both Wanda and Lucy were certain the sculptor was Ananda Kettering's great grandson, the descendant of the child that had been born in Chicago, a child Ananda had been told was stillborn. Lucy believed it would help the spirit to know her baby had lived to have children of her own. Wanda told him she'd prayed over it. In her mind they needed to try everything they could to help Madison by helping the woman who had drowned to find peace.

Two days ago he would have said it all sounded like a bunch of nonsense, but what could he say now after finding the poem? It seemed to him science had always been adversarial to the idea of an afterlife, but in the past few years he'd noticed more scientists were acknowledging the fact that they didn't have all the answers. The more mankind learned about the nature of the universe and quantum mechanics, the more they realized how mysterious and amazing it really was. Perhaps his father was right after all in his belief of the supernatural.

When he returned to Eagle Bay, he went directly to his office to check his schedule. Shelly, Linda's secretary was waiting for him with a list of questions when he stopped by. She also informed him he had a new patient. Someone by the name of Vincent Strickland had made an appointment. *Vincent Strickland?* Was it the same young man who had been in the room with him visiting Madison the first time she'd spoken out? Collin was certain it was.

Upon returning home, he found his silver laptop and Madison's notebook. When he carried them both to the kitchen table, he accidentally dropped the spiral notebook on the wood floor as he arranged his workspace. He bent over to pick it up and stared at the page that had fallen open. His heart picked up speed! How did he miss seeing it? *Nick forgive me, but I'm starting to have feelings for him!* It was only one sentence. It looked as though she had started to write a letter to her dead husband.

He took Goliath for a walk half hoping Robert McDuff would show up again out of the blue like he had several times before so he could talk to him. Sometimes he thought Robert was tailing him. Or was it just coincidence that Robert had shown up in several locations where he went? At first he found it annoying. Now he'd grown quite fond of the Scotsman. He actually missed him the past several days he'd been gone.

It was two hours later when he was finally at the hospital that he was informed that Madison had been moved to another room. Wanda was sitting in a chair in the corner reading a book when he entered.

"How is she?" he asked, studying Madison. He realized the dark circles under her eyes had only gotten more pronounced since he last saw her. He also noticed someone had slipped a child's teddy bear into the bed next to her that had a big red bow on it. He smiled when he saw the stuffed animal. There were a number of floral arrangements on the table next to Madison and one on the window sill with a balloon.

"She's about the same," Wanda said, pausing for a moment "Thank you so much for coming, Collin" She lowered her voice to a whisper. "Lucy and Robert should be here soon."

Minutes later Lucy walked into the room. Her cap of gray curls framed a somber face, yet her eyes were filled with hope. This will work, I just know it, Wanda," she said.

They heard someone cough in the hallway.

"Well you should know these things, I believe you are very much a psychic my dear Reverend Claremont," Robert gently teased as poked his head in the room for a moment then sat down on a chair in the hallway just outside the door.

"The outcome will be what we've been hoping for, Robert. I'm confidant of that. Madison will return to us and Ananda will find her way!"

"Aye, my lady, that's what we all need to believe."

"Robert, I told Father Gilbert what we're attempting to do. Wanda said, raising her voice a little. "He didn't say much, only to keep him posted and he would come if needed. I'm sure he's concerned about where this is going.

"There are certainly many Catholics who believe in ghosts. How could they not?" Robert stood in the doorway now. "Lucy is only acting as a mediator in this sense, trying to help Madison become free of a spirit that is troubling her."

"And Ananda is not an evil spirit! She's a poor woman whose soul is lost, caught in the "in between" in a state of fear because of her death," Lucy's eyes were filled with determination.

Now my dear," Lucy said, moving to Madison's bedside and taking her hand in her own, "we need you to help us convince Ananda to go to the light like she should've a long time ago." She leaned forward, her demeanor more determined than ever as she held Madison's hand. She gently smoothed the hair off of the younger woman's face.

Madison began to moan.

Collin walked over to her bed and put his hand on Lucy's

shoulder. When Lucy looked up at him he could make out the lines in her face. It was etched with worry.

Once again Madison moaned. She opened her mouth. Then she let out a scream that sent shivers down Collin's spine. It made the hair on his arms stand up. *Was she in pain? Was it Madison or Ananda who cried out?* Thoughts raced through his head as his heart picked up speed. He was a psychologist, he reminded himself. How could he possibly believe they were dealing with a ghost? And yet here he was in this hospital room with two women who were trying to exorcize a ghost or rather as Robert explained it, "get a spirit to understand she's dead and go to the light."

"I can assure you it's Ananda," Lucy said, reading his mind.

Within minutes of the scream a nurse appeared in the doorway. Moving towards the bed she quickly checked Madison's vital signs. Finally she turned to Wanda, "use the call button if you need help again,." she said.

"Thank you," Wanda said, "we certainly will."

Just then Oliver Whitestone appeared in the doorway. He was a very large muscular man with ruddy features and long black hair that was tied back in a pony tail. For several moments he stood in the doorway staring at the hospital bed where Madison was lying quietly now. "I'm sorry it took so long for me to get here," he finally said, nodding at Collin. Then he looked at Wanda and Lucy." How is she?"

"Madison's very weak," Lucy said in a soft voice. "And Ananda is agitated and afraid. She's also filled with anger at what happened to her. We have to make her understand who you are, Oliver. We have to help her understand that you are her great grandson. It will help her find peace."

"I believe she also wants her husband," Collin finally offered, watching Madison grimace again. "Ananda was going home to him when the ship foundered. John Baptiste was your great grandfather, Oliver. When he was a baby his mother called him Bitter Waters because he had colic and never stopped crying. He saved fourteen men in a terrible storm on November 9th 1873 when the schooner the Lydia B floundered near Eagle Bay. He was quite a hero."

Oliver's face was filled with questions. "How do you know all of this?"

Collin pulled out his cell phone. He found the photos he'd taken the day before on South Manitou Island and showed them to Oliver.

"The first one is a picture of his grave and the next one is of the poem your great grandmother wrote for him. It's quite beautiful even though it's sad. She loved him very much. But they were kept apart after your grandmother was conceived."

"But why?"

"Because he was a half-breed. That's what they called them back then," Collin explained. "His mother was a full blooded Chippewa. The lumber baron in town had an affair with her and left her pregnant with his child. Blue Goose became an alcoholic after this man promised her the world and left her on her own to fend for herself and the baby. Ananda, who we believe was your great grandmother, was the daughter of the town's doctor. John, your great grandfather was Blue Goose's child. John and Ananda played together when they were children. They eventually fell in love. When Ananda found out she was pregnant, they were secretly married by the priest who helped to raise John Baptiste after his mother tried to kill herself."

"How can I help them both?" Oliver asked, his hand automatically touching the little leather bag at his throat.

"Come sit here, Oliver," Lucy whispered, standing up at Madison's bedside.

Oliver walked over to the blue chair that Lucy had just vacated and sat down. He looked up at her, his black eyes questioning and somber.

"Now take her hand in yours. Let her feel your presence. You exist because of this woman, Oliver. I believe she'll understand that you've come here to help her find peace. We are all connected, Oliver. We are connected in spirit, and in the flesh when we are alive. You have her DNA and many people believe that our very cells store the memories of our ancestors. I believe she will know you."

Once again Madison grimaced as Oliver touched her. "Noooo!" she screamed, and began to moan.

Oliver withdrew his hand at once.

Lucy put her own hand on Oliver's shoulder. "Take a deep breath and relax. We must keep trying for Madison's sake."

Once again Oliver took Madison's hand. And once again she let out a scream that made Collin grit his teeth.

"Thank goodness we're in a private room," Wanda exclaimed. She got up from the chair and walked over to the foot of the bed. "Ananda, we need you to leave Madison alone now, dear. You need to go home to your husband and child," she pleaded.

Lucy put her ear close to Madison's mouth. "She's trying to say something," she said, turning her face towards Wanda.

"Suddenly Madison threw her head back as though gasping for air.

"Press the call button Lucy! She can't breathe! Something is terribly wrong!" Wanda cried.

WHEN EDEN REYNOLDS ARRIVED AT THE HOSPITAL, she found Wanda, Lucy and Oliver sitting in the waiting room. They were waiting for the nurse to give them the *all clear*. Eden took one look at Oliver and tried not to wince. *What is he doing here?* She quickly hurried past Oliver and sat down next to Wanda. She glanced at Oliver again and caught his eye, trying hard not to wince again. The image of the sculptor in Madison's apartment mutilating her friend's paintings wouldn't leave her mind.

She stood up. "Wanda, can I speak to you out in the hall for a minute?" she finally asked.

"Of course, dear," Wanda said, getting up herself.

Oliver stared at them as they filed past.

When they were out in the hall, Eden couldn't contain herself. "Oliver may be dangerous, Wanda!"

"Dangerous? But why?"

"Oliver's medicine pouch…" The words stuck in her throat.

"What about the medicine pouch, Eden? Oliver is here to help Madison. If he's not, maybe we should talk to Oliver!."

"You need to hear this. I think Oliver may have been responsible for destroying some of Madison's paintings!"

Wanda covered her mouth for a moment. Madison never said anything! Dear Jesus! Her paintings…? Why do you think it was Oliver?"

"Because Madison found the medicine bag lying on her floor the same night she found several of her paintings mutilated."

"Why didn't she tell me?"

"She didn't want you to worry. Madison thought it was Vincent who did it because she turned down his marriage proposal. But that night she found Oliver's medicine pouch on the carpet in the living room with the paintings."

"Did she call the police?

"No. She didn't want Vincent arrested."

"I don't know what to do, Eden. Oliver is here tonight because we asked him to come! Lucy believes he can help Madison."

"But how?" Eden glanced over Wanda's shoulder. Her face grew pale.

"Eden are you alright?"

"Not at this very moment," Eden said, putting her hand to her throat.

"What's wrong?"

"Vincent is here too."

Wanda turned and caught a glimpse of a lone figure at the far end of the hall approaching them.

"I think we should call security!" Eden turned and began to walk the other way towards the nurse's station, which was at the opposite end of the hall. Wanda quickly came up behind her and grabbed her elbow."

"Eden, Vincent being here may be a good thing...."

"I don't understand. How can he possibly help her?"

Lucy told me Madison spoke out for the first time the day Vincent came to visit her. I believe we have to have faith that things are working out as they should."

SOMETHING HAD TO BE WRONG! He'd been sitting in the lobby for over an hour waiting for a call from Wanda to let him know it was alright to go back up to Madison's room. Collin picked up his cell phone and quickly tried her number. It immediately went to voice mail. She must've turned it off! He stood up, chucked his empty foam cup in the garbage can and headed for the elevator.

When he got to the third floor he walked to the waiting room where he'd last seen Wanda, Lucy and Oliver. The room was completely empty now. *Why didn't they call him?* He started down the hallway. Turning the corner he could see that the door to Madison's room was shut. As he drew closer he heard faint voices on the other side. The muscles on his face and neck tightened with apprehension as he knocked and waited for the door to be opened. When Wanda's face finally did appear, she put a finger to her lips and motioned him towards the bed. The sight made him gasp. The young man whom he knew to be Vincent Strickland was leaning over Madison's bed whispering something to her while Lucy stood next to him watching quietly. *What in blue blazes was going on?*

"Madison, I'm sorry," Vincent pleaded. "I didn't mean to hurt you."

"Madison flung her head from side to side. "Please help me!" she pleaded. Her voice grew louder. "John, I'm so sorry for all of this. I'm so sorry! PLEASE HELP ME!"

Collin realized Oliver Whitestone and a very uncomfortable looking younger lady who he remembered was Madison's friend, Eden, were standing in the corner of the room between Wanda's chair and the wall. Shock and disbelief were written all over Eden's face.

Lucy appeared to watch the scene play out for several minutes before she motioned to Oliver who handed her his leather pouch. Lucy slowly withdrew something from the bag, and handed it to Vincent who gently nodded at her before taking Madison's hand in his own.

Collin's heart skipped a beat. *What exactly was going on here?*

After slipping a small gold wedding band on Madison's finger, Vincent quietly stepped back from the bed while Lucy took his place. She held Madison's hand in her own.

"Ananda? Do you remember this ring? It's the ring your husband gave you when you and he were secretly married. Your husband wants you to know that he's waiting for you. You're safe now. No one is going to hurt you."

The air in the room suddenly became very cold. Collin watched in amazement and apprehension as Madison jerked her hand away from Lucy's. She began to tremble violently. Every muscle in her body was twitching. *Was she having a seizure?*

"Sweet Jesus," Wanda said, getting up to press the call button again. Wanda's face was ashen.

"Wait!" Lucy put her hand up to stop Wanda. "I believe she's starting to understand. We don't need an interruption now."

Collin couldn't contain himself any longer. We need to call a nurse in here, stat, Wanda!"

Lucy took Madison's hand in her own. "No! We must wait. Someone else in the room could change the dynamics. It could frighten her even more. Ananda won't leave Madison if she's still afraid."

"Ananda, my dear, it's time to go," Lucy pleaded. "You must leave this young woman. She will die if you stay with her any longer. You need to go home to your husband and child now."

Collin could feel cold air filling the room. Madison began to tremble again. Her face became a mask of pain as the seizure grew in intensity.

CHAPTER TWENTY EIGHT

Collin walked along the concrete pier as a few flakes of snow fluttered around him. The wind stung his face while the moisture in his breath crystallized in the cold air. When he got to the small lighthouse at the end of the breakwater, he leaned against the base of the building and gazed out over the steel grey water that was frosted with whitecaps. He felt as gloomy as the day was dark.

When he'd left the hospital five days ago, Madison had been placed on a respirator. She'd stopped breathing after experiencing a seizure that had lasted more than five minutes. After waiting several hours to find out what happened, one of the doctors finally explained that Madison's organs had started to shut down. She had come into the hospital a healthy thirty four year old woman in a state of unconsciousness they were never fully able to understand and now she was declining rapidly. They could find no apparent reason for her condition and were completely baffled.

Lucy Claremont was not at all baffled by Madison's condition. She had explained to them that Madison had experienced the spirit's energy for too long and it had depleted her physically.

Collin took a deep breath. It was cold, but he needed the cold air to keep him awake. He had gotten very little sleep the night before. And he hadn't had any breakfast.

He walked back to his car. He was shivering as he opened the door of his Navigator and started the engine. Twenty minutes later, he pulled up to Clancy's Grill several blocks away from the gallery and parked his SUV. Sitting down at one of the tables in the restaurant that had been positioned under a group of old photographs of Eagle Bay, he placed his order when a pretty young waitress with blue streaks in her hair appeared by his side. While checking his text messages, he glanced up to see Robert McDuff looking down at him.

"I was hoping you would notice me soon, my friend," Robert said giving him a nod and a smile. "May I join you?"

"Of course, Robert. Be my guest. I see that you trimmed your beard again."

"Yes, my man, I did indeed. A little tired of young folks running up to me and sitting in my lap lately."

"Have you heard anything, Robert?"

"She's the same, I'm afraid. I just talked to Wanda on my cell." Robert paused. "Madison's in the "in-between" now my friend. I believe she's sorting it all out. Trying to decide whether to return to us and live again."

"Robert, Lucy told us Madison was having these physical problems and was in a state of altered consciousness because of Ananda's spirit, but she was not on the verge of dying like she is now. The doctors say her body is shutting down. She's actually in a real coma at this point. How can she possibly have control over anything? It will be up to her medical team to keep her alive and bring her out of this."

"I agree the doctors have a job to do. Madison's experienced the trauma Ananda experienced before she died and it's exhausted her physically as well as mentally." Robert frowned. "I can't imagine what it was like for her to experience the lives of all those people during the war night after night when she was a young girl."

"Robert, what do you mean?"

"Madison had nightmares when she was a young girl. Did she not tell you that? Wanda told me she'd awaken in the middle of the night for over a year crying when she was a young one. This was after her parents had died in the car accident of course. Madison told Wanda things that she saw in her dreams that no child that age should ever know about."

"What kind of things?

"Experiments that were done on people during the war in the concentration camps. The odd thing was she shouldn't have known about these things at that age. She was only eleven at the time.

Everyone had done what they could to shield her as much as possible. Joseph spoke very little to anyone about what happened to him and what he'd seen during the war. He was always careful to speak in Polish if he did talk to Wanda about something. Madison did not know the language. She could not have understood what they were saying, nor did she know the people she dreamt about, but Joseph did."

"How did Joseph deal with it?"

Madison didn't really understand what she was drawing at the time. But Joseph did. Her grandfather found it shocking that she could see the past so clearly even though he had tried to shield her from it. Joseph made her focus on her artwork to fill her mind with beautiful things. He also taught her to focus on the goodness in life. That's when she started to do her wonderful oil paintings. She was quite a prodigy when a child. At thirteen, so Wanda tells me, Madison was selling her paintings for thousands of dollars and helping her grandfather save for art school. By concentrating on her artwork she learned to control the nightmares that had been haunting her."

"It explains the Garden of Light."

"Ah, yes, the peace garden. She developed a foundation, hoping it would get off the ground one day." Robert paused and glanced up at the photographs on the wall above him. "Did you happen to see the beautiful collection of portraits she did of children from around the world that she hoped to place in the little museum in the peace park? The paintings are truly brilliant, Collin. The story goes that Madison confided in her aunt when she was a young girl that she dreamt of growing peace gardens in towns and cities all over the world. She called it the Garden of Light Project. I'd say the world could definitely use more peace."

Collin put his coffee cup down on the table. "I often wonder what the world would be like if the war had not happened?"

Robert shook his head sadly. "Ah that's a thing to be pondered. In the last seventy years it seems the world has become more brutal and heartless than it's ever been, and it's indeed been terrible at times. Look at what is happening in the Middle East right now. Besides what Hitler did, there were million of other souls who lost their lives because of Soviet communism, a style of government that didn't believe in any creator. Stalin and Hitler both believed in the supremacy of those who could take control by domination and force and has set into motion a chain reaction that is still going on today.

THE STEADY HUM OF THE MACHINES was the first thing he noticed when he stepped into the ICU. The second was the rubber hose that snaked into one of Madison's nostrils. Wanda sat in a chair by her bedside reading. He couldn't help but notice the profoundly dark circles under her eyes.

"I've been here all night. I went down to the chapel and prayed for the most part of it. I haven't slept if you're wondering why I look like this," Wanda said, standing up. She held her arms out to embrace him. "Thank goodness they're letting me stay in the room. I just can't leave her here alone like this."

"You look exhausted, Wanda," Collin said giving her a long hug. "You need to get some rest. Maybe you should go home for a while. I have a couple of appointments, but they're later this afternoon. I can spare a few hours here if it makes you feel better. I'll call you right away if there are any changes."

Wanda finally agreed. "I guess I'll be no use to her if I get sick myself. Perhaps a few hours will do me some good. I do need to take a shower. I'll come back at three then?"

"I think that would work out just fine." Collin gave her a tired smile. "I'll just get my book from the truck."

For two hours he sat reading the *Holographic Universe* while the clock on the wall above his head ticked away the minutes. At two twenty he started to doze. The dream couldn't have lasted more than a few minutes. But in it he was surprised to find Madison gesturing him to follow her down a winding path to what he knew was a beach. When she came to the end of the sandy trail she put her finger to her lips and pointed up. The night sky above them was filled with brightly shining constellations and the moon hung full and bright over the water as he walked up to her. When he noticed that she was shivering, he put his arm around her shoulders to keep her warm. For several moments they stood watching as the sun appeared on the horizon. As the glowing disk rose higher and higher in the sky, the sun exploded above their heads in a brilliant show of dazzling light and colorful fireworks. It startled him awake to the sound of machines humming and beeping. He quickly glanced over at the hospital bed. Madison was lying there as still as she was when he first walked in. But he sensed something had changed. He couldn't figure out what it was. Nor could he let go of the feeling that she had been standing over him when he'd been sleeping. It was an odd sensation.

At three thirty Wanda returned. She told him she'd showered and put on some clean clothes, besides doing a few things around the house. She thanked him and he said goodbye before leaving and driving to the office. He had several appointments that afternoon. One of them was with Vincent Strickland.

IT WAS THREE IN THE MORNING when the ring tone on his phone went off and Goliath who was sleeping beside his bed starting barking. His first thought was that Madison had taken a turn for the worse, but he was in complete shock when Robert told him she had disappeared from her room at the hospital.

"Madison is gone Collin! They can't find her anywhere!"

"Robert, how is that possible? She was hooked up to a respirator!"

Robert tried to catch his breath. "It just so happens that at around nine o'clock last night, Madison showed signs of movement in her toes. Wanda called me and Lucy to let us know. She was overjoyed! About an hour later, our dear lady moved her hand and tried to remove her respirator. Wanda was elated. For the last two days she's been in such a deep coma…"

"How could she have possibly left the hospital without anyone seeing her? How did she go from dying to getting out of bed in a matter of hours? None of this makes any sense, Robert."

"It doesn't make sense to the doctors either. Everyone is looking for her. Somehow she managed to find some clothes. She also left the hospital without anyone seeing her. Wanda called Lucy when they couldn't find her anywhere. They finally drove to Madison's apartment. She must've gotten a key somehow. Her car is not there."

"Where could she have gone?"

That's why I'm calling, my dear man. Were there any places that were special to her that she might've mentioned to you?"

"I'm completely at a loss, Robert, but I'll get dressed and help look for her. I'll give you a call if I think of something."

HE FOUND HER SITTING INSIDE HER MUSTANG with the motor running by the lighthouse. When he tapped on the window to get her attention there was no response at first. Then she slowly turned to look at him.

"Madison," he said, "please open the door." He pointed at the lock and was relieved when he heard it pop open. "Are you okay? You gave us all a very big scare today."

She didn't answer. She turned to look out the windshield again. Finally when he was on the verge of reaching in the car to touch her, she gave him a sad smile and then looked down. He realized she was finally opening the door. He instinctively took a few steps back to make room for her to get out.

"When they didn't find you at the hospital, I guessed that you would come here," he said when she was standing in front of him..

"I'm sorry for putting everyone through this," she said softly.

Emotion welled up inside of him. "I care about you Madison. Everyone has been so worried."

She glanced at the ground for a moment. Then she lifted her chin to look up at him. Her blue eyes were shining with tears.

"Do you *know* what happened to you?" he asked gently.

"I've been asleep...but I actually haven't been sleeping."

He raised an eyebrow trying to comprehend her meaning.

"You prayed over his grave, Collin. I know it helped them both,"

He let out a small gasp. "How did you know?"

"John didn't think anyone cared about him or Ananda."

"Father Chabert cared about him."

"He always knew that. But everyone else treated him so badly because he was in love with Ananda. He knew that he and Ananda were meant to be together since they were children. He told me they were connected by something sacred and no one could sever that bond."

Without another word she walked towards the beach. He followed her down a sandy path that wound between two small dunes covered with shrubs. He could hear waves hitting the concrete revetment in front of the lighthouse. When they made their way past the vegetation that hid their view of the lake, Madison stopped and gazed up at the sky. Collin felt a knot grow in his throat as he watched her sit down on a wooden bench that faced the lake and finally lift her hand to look at the wedding ring that Vincent had placed on her finger in the hospital. He was surprised she was still wearing it. He walked up to her and sat down.

"Collin, I never told you this in therapy," she paused, searching for words. "When I was a little girl, I had dreams," she whispered. "They were nightmares actually.

In the faint light he could see purple shadows under her eyes. *How did she ever have the strength to get out of bed and drive?* He wondered. "Robert told me about them, Madison. He said you were up every night for several months after your parents died."

Madison swallowed. "I guess I was afraid to tell you about them in therapy. I buried the memory deep inside me for so long even though it was my grandfather's secret. You see, one night when I was a child, after my parents died, I had a dream that was so awful that when I woke up I couldn't stop sobbing or get back to sleep. My grandfather held me in his arms most of the night. He slept in the chair in my bedroom so he could watch over me."

"The next morning, I was able to tell him about the dream without breaking into tears." Madison covered her face with her hands for moment. Finally she looked at him. "I told him that I'd dreamt I'd been lying face down on a wooden floor. I remember feeling the side of my head ache. And my eyes were burning. I could also smell urine. I felt something warm oozing down the side of my face. I ran my hand over my forehead and felt a huge gash over my right eye. I realized it was blood. I was so scared that I began to heave, but there was nothing in my stomach, because I knew I hadn't eaten in three days. Without warning. two men entered the room just then. They were wearing uniforms. I remember one of them being very handsome, but having electric blue eyes that were cold and cruel. The soldiers grabbed me under each arm and tried to stand me up several times, but I would collapse onto the floor. One time I hit my head so hard that I saw stars. Finally, when I couldn't stand up again they began to kick and punch me. Then they each took a leg and dragged me across the floor to the doorway and down some concrete steps. My head kept smashing against the ground. I remember they took me to a cellar where they tied me to a chair." Her voice trailed off.

For several moments they sat silently watching the beacon sweep the sky above them. Collin finally cleared his throat. "Let's go back to your car and sit inside and talk, Madison," he finally whispered. "You must be cold." He stood up and waited for her to follow him. He could feel the frigid air bite at his face. He was thankful they had both worn winter jackets.

Without another word she slipped off the bench and started down the path back to the parking area. He followed her.

Opening the door of her car, she tucked herself in the front seat and started the engine. .

"Can I ask you something?" Collin blew on his hands to warm them up when he got in the passenger seat. "How did you get home from the hospital?"

"One of the nurses that was on duty tonight was an art student of mine years ago. She was filling in for another nurse and was just leaving for home when I ran into her. She didn't know how sick I'd been. When I spotted her in the hallway I told her my aunt was in the hospital and that I was having car problems and needed a ride home. She dropped me off at the house."

"I can't imagine how you escaped from all those tubes."

"She gave him a sad smile. I must take after my grandfather." Collin, I need to tell you the rest of the story, then maybe you'll understand.." She paused, finally taking another breath and continued. "After the men led me down the steps they tookme to a blood stained wall where I knew I was to be shot. That's when I woke up."

"You should have been dreaming about puppies and ponies at that age!"

"That's what my grandfather said when I told him about the nightmare. His hands shook terribly when he handed me my breakfast the next morning. He looked like he was going to be ill. He had been so upset. Years later I realized what a shock it must have been when I related such a horrible dream to him when I was such a young girl. He always tried to shield me from the brutality he had experienced. He never talked about the war in front of me."

Once again a tear slid down her cheek and she took a deep breath, drawing in the warmer air in the car. "You see, Collin, I found out years later that the dream had actually been about my grandfather. I had described in detail what he had experienced when he was a young man who had been caught by Nazi soldiers smuggling food to the prisoners in the concentration camp he had been interred in." She paused for a moment and took a breath. "He never mentioned this episode to anyone throughout his life including my aunt. He was just so guilt ridden about what he'd done."

"But why? He was very courageous. He was also a hero for trying to help others."

"It's true he was very brave, but he also may have been the cause of a multitude of deaths. The Poles were under threat of death for helping Jewish citizens. And that extended to their families. Collin, my grandfather's life had been spared because someone in the resistance had been able to bribe the guards. He escaped the firing squad, but when he returned to his village he found that everyone there had been gunned down by the Germans. His sister, two brothers and first wife, had all been shot. Only, my aunt Wanda, who was an infant at the time, had been left alive in her crib. He always believed it was because the guards had caught him burying burlap sacks filled with rotting vegetables under the barbed wire fences for the prisoners to eat. He kept his secret until he had a stroke and couldn't keep it any longer. He told me the story several days before he died. The memory of what happened so many years ago burned inside of him and haunted him all those years. How could he ever think of himself as a hero after knowing he had possibly caused the extermination of an entire village?"

"Why didn't you tell me this in therapy? You've been holding these sad memories inside for so long, just like your grandfather."

"I'm sure there are millions of stories out there like my grandfather's that are untold. The Iron Curtain suppressed the voices of the Poles when the communists took over after the war. Many Polish citizens were sent to gulags if they had been in the resistance fighting against the Germans. They were tortured and starved, dumped off into the freezing tundra without food and shelter, having to fend for themselves if they didn't agree with the communist agenda for Poland. Then they were abused by people who thought they were partly to blame for the Holocaust." She rubbed her eyes for a moment and looked at him. "Here in the states so many people know about what happened to the Jews, but don't get the full story about what happened to the Catholics in

Poland."

Collin leaned closer to her. He reached for a strand of hair that fell over her eyes, accidentally brushing her lips with his fingers when he pushed it away.

She gave him a sad smile. "My grandfather was my hero, Collin. Every day I think about him and miss him. I miss his kindness and compassion, and most of all his wisdom and warmth. I guess there's so much more I need to tell you in therapy."

Reaching for her hand, he held it in his own. "There's something I also need to tell *you,* Madison." He cleared his throat. Linda will be returning to her practice soon."

"Do you plan on moving back to Grosse Point to be closer to your son?"

"I've been thinking about it. I've also had something else on my mind. I have reservations about telling you this, but I feel it's the right thing to do." He let out a breath. "Madison, I do care about you very much, in fact more than I should as your therapist. The big problem is I've fallen in love with you."

She let out a small gasp. "After everything that's happened?"

"None of it was your fault. I know about the paintings and why you didn't report Vincent."

She thought of the letter she'd started to write to Nick *Forgive me but I'm starting to have feelings for him.* She couldn't help her feelings for Collin. The way they'd been brought together. It was as though it had all been planned. The thought of not seeing him again filled her with sadness.

"Collin. I'm sorry for all I've put you through. But I'm not sorry I met you."

"Madison, you've filled my world with many surprises, not all of them bad. I've gotten to know you these past several months. I've gotten to know who you are and how you've tried to bring compassion and healing to the world even though you could be filled with bitterness and hatred because of what happened to your family. You're not like anyone I've ever met. Your presence has filled my life with beauty and sweetness." He paused and gave her a smile. "And especially art. I really needed something to go along with that sad lonely photograph of a tree in my office."

She didn't know what to say. He'd certainly touched her heart. Who else understood her as well as Collin? Not even Nick had been able to completely understand her heartache.

"Linda Bishop is coming back from Florida in a week. I told her that I'm thinking about leaving the practice and taking a teaching position at the college in Traverse City."

Her face was filled with questions.

What I'm getting at is that I want to spend more time with you, but not as your therapist.

"I still don't understand."

He cleared his throat. "Vincent came to see me several days ago. He confessed to mutilating your paintings. He also told me he dropped Oliver Whitestone's medicine bag on the floor in your apartment to make it look like Oliver had broken in. He said he was sorry for what he did. He gave me his permission to tell you how guilty he felt and that he was thankful you didn't call the police. He also told me he knew you weren't going to die."

"How? Why?"

"Very strangely Vincent told me he dreamt he was invited to your wedding."

She gave a small gasp. "My wedding? To whom?"

Collin squeezed her hand. "I really can't tell you, Madison, I believe that part is confidential."

"I never loved Vincent, Collin. He was always a friend, but nothing more. I know he's a good person down deep. What he did to my art work was very unfortunate. I'm sure he was drunk. I had planned to give the paintings he destroyed to a group home for a fundraiser. They had been in my closet for years."

Collin nodded. "I'm convinced he's sorry. He told me he would like to compensate you for the paintings."

Madison gave him a sad smile. "Please tell him I'd appreciate it. The group home could certainly use the money, so much funding has been cut in the state."

"I will. Madison, why did you leave the hospital so suddenly?"

"I felt claustrophobic in that small room. It reminded me of the dream I had of my grandfather. I just had to get out of there."

"Have the dreams about your grandfather stopped?"

"There really was only one dream about my grandfather. The rest of them were more than dreams."

"What do you mean?"

"Collin, about some of the experiences I've had as a child," she looked down at her hands for a moment again. "I didn't tell you about them in therapy." She paused searching for the right words. "What I'm trying to say is that some of the people who died during the war visited me when I was a child. They were traumatized by how they died. They needed someone to help them cross over to the light."

He wasn't surprised anymore at anything she told him. "Is that what happened with Ananda? Did her spirit come to you for help?"

"I didn't know what was happening at first. I thought the visits had stopped a long time ago. I hadn't experienced anything like that since I was a young girl. When I waded out to the wreckage, I realize now, I was overcome by Ananda's presence. That's why I lost my memory. Afterwards I began experiencing some very strange and confusing feelings that I thought were associated with Nick's death. I realize now those intense feelings of anger and despair were not all my own, they were Ananda's. All this time, I've been fighting to hold onto my sanity, because her feelings were filling up my consciousness. I couldn't hold her back."

"Is Ananda finally at peace?"

"When Oliver came to visit in the hospital, Ananda finally understood that her baby hadn't died at birth. When Vincent put John's ring on my finger she knew John was waiting for her. I saw them together."

"Did you see your husband too?"

"I might not have wanted to come back if I had. I think there was a reason for that. Nick told me he wanted me to be happy just before he died. He told me he wanted me to find someone else, because I still needed someone to help me with our plans. It was a surprise to me when I realized I had to return, because I really cared about you."

Collin drew in a breath.

She put her hand on his arm for a moment. "I've read the Holographic Universe, it's an interesting book. I saw you reading it when you were in my room. Do you think?"

Before she could finish her sentence, his mouth found his way to her lips. When they separated her eyes were filled with questions, and shining with tears.

"I'm sorry, Madison," Collin was contrite. "I shouldn't have done that."

"I've been wondering what that would feel like for quite some time. I didn't think I could care about anyone else after Nick died."

"Linda will be coming back soon," he whispered.

"What are you going to tell her?"

"I'll have to tell her that I'm in love with one of my patients. After what happened with Vincent, I don't want this making you feel uncomfortable, Madison. I will leave you alone if you want me to."

"Collin, I love everything about you. I love the kindness I see in your heart. I love how much you care about your patients. I don't know what I'd do without you, right now."

"I realized something extraordinary had happened in my life when I met you," Collin whispered.

"That first day when I saw you on the beach, I wanted to do a drawing of you. There was just something about you. Afterwards when you carried me to shore and I woke up, your eyes were filled with so much concern for me. I've learned to trust you, Collin. Your love for me is a gift."

"So can we conclude from that very first moment on the beach, that you've been drawn to me?"

"Collin Richardson, I was *drawn* to you from the moment I saw you." She paused, "that is, until our dear ghost came into my life near the wreckage and things got hairy. No telling what would have happened."

"Speaking of hairy," he said, brushing a strand of hair away from her mouth. "Goliath loves his new collar more than you can imagine. I think he actually struts when he walks now." Collin cleared his throat. "By the way, there is one thing that haunts me about all of this."

"Only one thing? I envy you that."

"What exactly happened to Ananda's body? The coroner did an autopsy on it. I would assume she'd be buried somewhere near Eagle Bay, but I haven't been able to locate her grave."

"Her body was stolen. Apparently the coroner did an autopsy on it and determined that she was still alive when the ship went down. It would have been quite a scandal to find out that she had been left in the rigging to die. It was the lake man's code to save women and children first. Apparently the crew of the Lydia had jumped into the water to save themselves, but left Ananda behind even though they knew she was still alive, because they were ordered to. She's buried in one of the dunes on the beach near where I was painting. I hope Oliver will agree to have her taken to the cemetery on South Manitou to be buried near John's grave. I know she would like that."

"Who buried Ananda there?"

"The man who attacked her on the ship had his men take her body from the morgue. He was the same man who caused the church to catch fire. That's where John actually died after the ship foundered. John was struck on the head by Ananda's attacker when he confronted him. A candle was knocked over in the church and a fire started. John was pulled out of the church before the fire got to him, but unfortunately he was overcome by smoke. So was Father Chabert. They both died of asphyxiation. I have a hunch that's why I've been getting splitting headaches at times. It seems Nathanial Burgess, John's attacker, had been in love with Lydia even though she was half his age. When he found out about her pregnancy he was filled with rage. He had some weird idea that Lydia was in love with him. I also don't think he knew that John was the son he had with Blue Goose. It all breaks my heart."

"I thought John died because of hyperthermia."

"Apparently that's what they told everyone. The truth is John's death was caused by his own father. Nathanial Burgess *was* his father, Collin."

"Nathanial is also Eden's great grandfather."

"Yes, I know. I'm not sure I want to tell Eden about all of this. I don't know how she'll take it."

"What an amazing and sad story."

"There was some good that came out of it. In spite of Nathanial, there's a great deal for Eden to be proud of, Collin. Lydia Burgess found out about Blue Goose. Eden's great grandmother eventually established a home for indigent women in the area. She was an extremely kind and generous woman. When Blue Goose had another child years later and the baby was born with disabilities Lydia provided care for her. Taki was John's half sister. Everyone thought she was mentally handicapped, but she was gifted with some amazing talents."

Collin nodded. "I read about her. It sounds like the child was an autistic savant. And a saint. Chabert recorded in his journal that she used to paint pictures of landscapes that were phenomenal. I guess Lydia encouraged them. He also wrote that deer and other animals used to follow her when she walked through the woods, and that she would talk to animals and they understood her. Some people claimed she actually was able to heal people. It sounds like beauty and the beast to me."

"It brings to mind something Nick used to say, that there are far more handicapped minds in the most intelligent people. I don't know what eventually happened to her, but I do know the world could use a little more beauty and innocence. Don't you?"

"I agree that there are far more ugly images on television than there needs to be. Crime shows and the news seem to focus on the bad in people. What you focus on does truly grow. Yet we can't stick our heads in the sand. There is so much destruction on this planet that we need to know about too."

"Oh I agree, I just wish."

"You're forgetting something, Madison."

"What's that?"

"John was Eden's great uncle. He saved all those crewmen when the ship was sinking. There were nine men in all. Many of those young sailors had actually bullied him because of his relationship with Ananda. John could have ignored their pleas for help, but he didn't. He showed a great deal of courage and compassion rescuing those men. "

"That's so true, Collin. There are bad people in the world, but I'd like to believe there are far more good people who struggle every day to set the world right by their love and compassion for others."

"Would you like me to drive you home tonight? You look exhausted. We can pick up your car tomorrow."

Madison nodded. "I think that would be a good idea. Not surprisingly, I do feel a bit drained. I just want to say thank you for everything, Collin with *two* L's, Richardson." She gave him a tired smile and put her hand gently on his cheek.

Collin took her hand. He cleared his throat. "Actually I should be thanking you Madison *Avenue* Andrews. You've restored my faith in humanity." For several moments he looked at her without saying anything. Finally letting go of her hand, he turned to gaze out the window at the night sky, remembering the dream he had in her hospital room. And the fireworks.

"I'd like to help you with your peace park," he finally said, turning back to her and gently touching the ring on her finger. *Would she actually wear a ring he gave her some day as Vincent Strickland's dream suggested?.* Madison's mouth curved into a smile. Collin could see her eyes glisten in the soft light of her car.

"I picture the park in my mind every day, Collin," she whispered. "I want to have interactive sculptures there. Maybe even a butterfly house for children. It will be a template for other parks in other places, in the world, perhaps, hopefully even in Detroit. We could possibly grow gardens in them filled with food that actually feed the homeless and use them as community service centers. I always imagined it to be an interfaith project with churches from each city contributing and working together to grow their own park. It could be a place where people go in each community to mourn and heal together. And just be happy."

"How about a section of the park devoted to dogs? We can't forget about Goliath." He gave her a smile. "It sounds like a lot of work, but every idea starts with someone planting the seeds." Once again he gently took her hand. "It'll take me a while to arrange things, but I'm positive I can help you. My aunt actually has a foundation. She lives in Grosse Pointe in one of those big fancy houses on Jefferson Avenue near the Ford Estate and the Yacht Club. She and my Uncle started it years ago. After he died she's asked me numerous times to manage it for her. I think now's the time I told her I would."

DENISE COUGHLIN

For more information on Poland's Forgotten Holocaust,

books to read are,

Forgotten Holocaust

The Poles under German Occupation, by Richard G. Lukas, with

forward by Norman Davis

Also

Bloodlands

Europe between Hitler and Stalin

By Timothy Snyder

Irena Sendler

Mother of the Children of the Holocaust

By

Anna Mieszkowska

ACKNOWLEGMENTS

I would like to thank my mom, Terry, for all of her encouragement and support throughout the process of writing this book. I want to thank the Shelby Writer's Group, especially Tony Aued, and Carl Vittiglio, for their very helpful suggestions while putting this story together, besides Author Alexandra Tesluk Gibson. My husband Ken's love of Great Lakes nautical history has always been an inspiration to me and helped me develop this work of fiction. His technical support was invaluable to me. My thanks and appreciation also go to Mary Kay, the author of *How To Be Psychic,* for her expert advice and to Carol and Gerry Turgeon for their help with editing. Much appreciation goes to my friend, and fellow visionary, Sharon Sigler, for her encouragement and belief in the *dream.*

AUTHOR BIOGRAPHY

Denise Coughlin is an artist, public speaker and author who has written several books for children, among them *Dragon In My Pocket* and *Daniel Cullpepper and the Case of the Hyperpotamus*. This is Denise's first novel for adults. She's enjoyed writing since she was a little girl and has spent her life on the Great Lakes boating with her family and exploring Michigan's natural beauty. Her love of her home state, it's Native American Legends, and Maritime history, inspired her to write Bitter Waters. She is working on another book for adults, entitled *My Fathers Tears; Memoir of a Survivor's Daughter, One Woman's Journey of Faith, Healing and Miracles.*